MR THISTLEWOOD

By the same author

Fiction

Jupiter Laughs
Pharaoh's Chicken
The Tale Bearer
Eclipse

Travel

Handles of Chance
China in the Morning
Red Rumba
Winter in England

Biography

The Man on the Ice Cap

MR THISTLEWOOD

Nicholas Wollaston

Hamish Hamilton
London

First published in Great Britain
by Hamish Hamilton Ltd
Garden House 57-59 Long Acre
London WC2E 9JZ

British Library Cataloguing in Publication Data
Wollaston, Nicholas
  Mr. Thistlewood.
  I. Title
  823'.914[F]   PR6073.045
  ISBN 0-241-11585-X

Typeset at The Spartan Press Ltd, Lymington, Hants
Printed in Great Britain by St Edmundsbury Press Ltd,
Bury St Edmunds, Suffolk

I met Murder on the way –
He had a mask like Castlereagh –
Very smooth he looked, yet grim;
Seven blood hounds followed him.

*

Clothed with the Bible, as with light,
And the shadows of the night,
Like Sidmouth, next, Hyprocrisy
On a crocodile, rode by.

SHELLEY

from *The Mask of Anarchy*,
written on
the occasion of the massacre
at Manchester,
August 16th 1819.

Paris 1792–London 1820

. . . I see a young man on the hot straight road to Paris, travelling from Calais. Fresh from the channel boat, abroad for the first time. A summer day, a grave young man drawn by the events ahead. A few books in his baggage, a few gold guineas, a few ideas. The wide hedgeless cornfields, the novelty. August 1792, nearly thirty years ago.

Everyone was coming the other way. Along the road were carriages flying from the capital. When I stopped for lunch the waiter spoke of a secret conspiracy due to break out on the tenth of August – today was the ninth. I didn't understand properly, my French was bad and I laughed at a secret that was public knowledge. But at each town down the road the rumours got firmer. Things were going to happen, people told me – Paris was about to blow up, I was mad to go there. Others said there was no danger for a foreigner. The king would lose his crown and that was too bad, he had it coming to him – nothing to worry a tourist. They packed up and drove north to the English channel. Some to Belgium, they said. Most of them were in their own carriages, they hadn't hired them. The boss class. Family parties, fine ladies, pretty children. Superior clothes, manners, voices. The same as the ones in England but with an extra quality, a disdain that I didn't like . . . I see the contempt in the women's eyes. Perhaps it was only because they were foreigners to me, and frightened. I watched them go, then continued down the road. A heavy summer afternoon, a slumbering torpor, a presentiment over the face of France. A young man on his way to Paris. The national guard who stopped me at the Porte St Denis was my age. He asked to see my passport and tried to pronounce the name, then waved me on. Arthur Thistlewood – not easy on a French tongue. Not really such a young man, just twenty-one. Not even innocent, but on fire.

. . . I see the hotel in Paris. I had been given the address and took a cab there. The Hôtel de Moscovie behind St Germain. A tourist district, but that's what I was, and I didn't know I would stay two years. In time my room became a meeting place. I bought books and kept stacks of newspapers and pamphlets. Any important speech in parliament was ordered to be printed, I still have most of them . . . I see the parties we had in that room, arguing through the night. We felt important, and we were. Since then, when I have been in Paris I go back to the Hôtel de Moscovie. It hasn't changed, it's still run by the same family, but Clothilde is now in charge. Ah, Clothilde! – I tried for two years but it was no use. My friends laughed and said it was just as well, she would make me marry her and turn me into a bourgeois husband. She was treacherous like them all, they said, and when I look at the gigolo she has got . . . I see that first night in Paris as if it were last month, not thirty years ago.

The tenth of August. I wonder what quirk of chance brought me to Paris on that date and how different my life would have been if I had arrived a day later. I'm fascinated by the little accidents, the twists that have brought me to this dingy London tenement.

I went to bed early with my window open to the hot street, but at midnight I was woken by drums and shouts. The landlord came into my room in a panic – Clothilde's father – and said that everyone must keep their windows lit. Clothilde brought a lamp and put it on my table, the flame in her eyes. I got my clothes on and went down to the street, I could never sleep again. Crowds everywhere and soldiers, torches, drummers. The Pont Neuf was a mass of national guards, the Pont Royal was solid, I couldn't cross the river. This was the secret conspiracy I had been warned about on the road from Calais. Someone called 'Monsieur Thistlewood' behind me – Clothilde had followed me. I fell in love by the Pont Royal. We were up all night, pressed together in the crowd. She didn't know who they were – from Brittany and Marseille, not Paris. It was because the king had used his veto against the parliament and was defending the priests who wouldn't take the oath for the new constitution. At dawn the bells began to ring – the tocsin, Clothilde said. They might have been ringing for us. The way she held my hand and talked about the king and priests, her breasts rising to me . . . I see the rapture on a young man's face, the lust pulsing through his fingers, and my blood still quickens.

We went back to the hotel for breakfast. My first Paris morning. Clothilde's father would have been angry with us for staying out all night if he hadn't been so agitated. He ran to the window, out into the street, upstairs to look out over the roof, down again to see if anyone had broken in. Locking doors, fussing into closets. He was afraid someone might get into the cellar, at his wine. Mistrust in all his movements. Clothilde only laughed at my bad French.

The guns began at about nine. Cannon-fire from the other side of the river. Then shouts went up the street, window to window, house to house. Men running, half frantic with delight, half with misery. 'They're shooting at us, we're being killed!' Yelling, howling at the outrage. Clothilde looked at her father. She was eighteen. 'The palace has been attacked, they're firing back!' People rushed in and out, up and down. 'Citizens, to arms!' It's true, it's what they shouted. Clothilde looked at me. Without a word we were in the street again, marching to the palace with the citizens of Paris, sucked into the stream. There was only one way to go, we swam for all we could, clutching each other for our lives. National guards, armed citizens, pikemen joined the flood – it was that or drowning. Marching, flowing to the palace. Some were dragging cannons. We found a backwater from the torrent by the Pont Royal where the street widened and we could stop.

. . . I see the palace across the river. The royal family inside, where they had lived since they were caught escaping last year and brought back to Paris in shame. The king, queen, prince and princess, a few courtiers, guarded by a Swiss battalion in the barracks next door. As we stood there, Clothilde and I among the breathless crowd by the Pont Royal, three men ran out of the palace towards the river – towards us. Someone shouted, someone fired, a volley broke from the national guards and the fleeing men fell before they reached the middle of the bridge. The citizens yelled. Our cannons were hauled on to the bridge and opened up. At the first shot the women screamed and clapped: 'Bravo, the cannons!' Clothilde looked up with wonder on her face, and tears. Wasn't this incredible, marvell-

3

ous? We were firing at the king, knocking holes in his palace, salvo after salvo. The Swiss guards fired muskets from the windows, and citizens were hit. Some were killed, from the screams. We ducked under the parapet along the river and watched through the balustrade. Horsemen trampled through the crowd, platoons of national guards marched this way and that, telling us to go home – only those with guns should stay. But we crouched there while the cannons fired.

A big man with a chin like a ploughshare shouted, grabbed my shoulder, pulled me to my feet. The crowd thickened round us, pointing at me. Sticks and fists and dangerous old guns. I remembered the three dead men on the bridge just now. 'Aristocrat!' they shouted, their breath and spittle in my face, and jeered and prodded. The big man shook my coat, clenched his jaw, set his chin. Clothilde flew at him with teeth and nails: 'He's English!' They laughed – an Englishman was a harmless joke – and the man let go and slunk away.

The word went round that the king had left the palace. Hours ago, while we were having breakfast in the Hôtel de Moscovie, he had walked with his family through the gardens to the parliament and asked for protection. All morning we were shooting cannonballs at an empty palace. The Swiss guards were defending nobody but their fire was deadly, we must attack. It was my first day in Paris, I kept telling myself.

. . . I see the barracks in flames. The Swiss were butchered for being Swiss, for firing on the people, for defending a king who wasn't there. A king who wasn't theirs. He paid them twopence a day, then abandoned them. A twopenny king who enticed young soldiers from the Alps with promises of Paris, glory, girls. Some fled to join him in the parliament, some rushed into the streets and were chased and cornered. By the afternoon it was finished.

We went back to St Germain, to a café, and sat in the August sun. People were drinking, talking, dreaming. The palace had been stormed, the royal family had found shelter in parliament, a thousand citizens were dead, the waiter said. Later he corrected it: two thousand. Sometimes a squad of battle-drunk national guards came down the street, marching home with scarlet trophies stuck on their bayonets – bits of the Swiss guards' uniform. A lion-headed scowling old noble was dragged by in a carriage with a mounted escort – to the Abbaye,

Clothilde said. Next a lady, richly dressed, was taken on foot the same way. People in the café hardly noticed. I tried to seem nonchalant. Two days ago I had left England. But I wasn't the only Englishman, and there were three fair-headed students from Germany or Scandinavia, and an American shouting over the tables for another coffee. Clothilde said, 'Tell me about London,' but she didn't want to hear. To attack St James's Palace! 'Come on,' she said, 'let's go and see the victory.'

. . . I see the naked Swiss bodies lying in heaps round the palace, stripped and slashed on the terraces, in the gardens. Eight hundred out of a thousand had been killed, a woman said with satisfaction. The French dead had been taken away, the Swiss would be left till tomorrow. Their barracks were still burning. Now the palace gates were open and everyone was going in to look – mostly women. We walked through the great silent rooms and stared. The royal family had lived here till eight o'clock this morning and would never come back. People couldn't speak aloud after such slaughter. Clothilde took my hand, we followed the crowd up the staircase. A shriek from somewhere above, a great commotion at the top of the stairs. A minute later a dead man was carried down past us, pursued by shouts of scorn. He had been caught pinching some trinket of the queen's and killed on the spot. Clothilde said, 'The people's justice,' and I was glad of her hand in mine. The sovereign people.

On the third day after the palace attack I went to the Paris parliament. A foreigner could get a ticket, I found a seat among the members. The gallery was reserved for the claqueurs – hired, Clothilde said.

I felt less of a stranger there than I had in the English parliament. At Westminster I was a tourist too, a young man from Lincolnshire. I heard Pitt and Burke and Fox, sat through the rigmarole, watched the speaker drive the clanking machine along. That ageless figure in a wig and robes – Lord Sidmouth himself, the old grub, my life's enemy. At his feet were four men writing at a table with the golden prehistoric mace beside them. Beyond, four hundred of the most absurd men possible. Whispering, winking, lolling with drowsy eyes and tilted hats, overfed, drunk with boredom, some of them stiff with starch or pride. One was waving his arms, lost in speech, but nobody worried. The most illustrious assembly of free men in the world, making laws I must obey. It was like an aquarium. I was assailed by anger, I would commit a private act, standing up and shouting, 'I come from the north and if you sods down there knew about the people you think you rule . . . ' Two flunkeys had me pinioned, hauled me out, kicked me down into the street. They didn't march me off to Bow Street, I wasn't worth it. A silly youth with nothing better to do. Wait till he knows his place, learns some manners, finds a job. It wasn't in the papers next day, it had never happened. But there was something before the flunkeys stifled me that I remembered when I was outside. It lasted hardly a second, no more than the look a snake might give a fly, infinitely chilling and contemptuous. It contained an entire system of privilege and was meant for me alone. It came from Sidmouth in the speaker's chair.

The Paris parliament was another world, real and wild. Here was life, humour, passion. My little scene would have been a sneeze in this clamour. The members were noisy enough, jealous of anyone called to the tribune or anyone who heard the call, but the gallery was louder. Hoots, whistles, belches, even speeches from the public, mostly obscene. The ushers shouted for silence, the gallery shouted back. Fifty people were on their feet with fifty arguments. One member lost his temper and was storming the gallery alone when someone pulled him back, frightened of things getting worse. They were debating which church bells should be melted down to make money. The president's own bell was drowned. It was far from the irrelevance of Westminster and the icicle Sidmouth eyes.

. . . I see the royal family sitting below the president in a little panelled box. For three days they had lived there, with nothing to do but listen. A man and wife, a small boy and girl, the man's sister, one or two friends, the governess and a beautiful lady-in-waiting, a fairy-tale princess. A kingdom was reduced to that little box.

After the church bells were dealt with a cannoneer was brought to the bar, a square man with a beard, famous for the hits he had scored on the palace and the silver teapot he had saved from it. Solemnly he put it on the table. More followed – clocks, pictures, china, furniture, candlesticks and crucifixes from the chapel, rescued from the looters. A ragged tramp brought a jewelbox, a national guardsman came with his hat full of gold coins. The gallery cheered, the royal family watched nervously from their box like expensive toys in a shop, also saved from damage, waiting for someone to buy them. I imagined our raddled English king in that box, with the dreadful dukes and blowsy women. A man shouted, 'The bloodshed of the tenth of August is the work of that traitor!' and pointed venomously at the king. He would have spat if he could reach. Someone added, 'And all the miseries of France!' The children looked up at the burst of cheering, but the king and queen sat like dummies, dolls, puppets, not a quiver, and the lady-in-waiting only flushed. When a member went to the tribune and demanded that the king should quit the throne the gallery laughed. Not cheers, not boos, only laughter.

I told Clothilde about it at the Hôtel de Moscovie that night. The king looked a fool, the queen a prig, but not dangerous. They whispered in the debate and leant forward to follow a speech, or passed round biscuits and sipped lemonade. The children fidgeted and were told off. But Clothilde laughed like the gallery. She had never seen the king and queen, she was annoyed that I could be bothered, I wasn't a real revolutionary, they were villains who had killed two thousand Frenchmen and deserved all that was coming. I tried to tell her about the momentousness, the sense of struggle, my compulsion to take part, the way I felt men's minds could be exalted above the selfishness of life as well as abased beyond the depths, and the feeling of great virtue and great vice, of a chance for a new nobility to be born. I couldn't explain it in my French. Clothilde laughed again and kicked her foot from under her skirt. It was nothing to do with nobility, she said, nobility was dead. But that was what I meant. I never believed that a poor man couldn't be heroic, generous, wise. Anybody could, who was capable of enthusiasm – you didn't have to be young, though it was better, and you could call it love. It was the minions of fortune, the men with stagnant minds, the pampered children of luxury and profusion, who were damned. But I didn't know half the words, and still Clothilde laughed. I took her by the shoulders and shook her till she stopped, till her hair flew about her head and her breasts wobbled in her bodice. I could have ripped it down and pulled them out and pushed her back on my bed and raped her. Did I never make love to Clothilde? My fantasies were so real, I can't be sure. Sometimes I brought a prostitute back from a St Germain café, hoping that

7

Clothilde would discover. All night, every time I fucked her, I caught her tongue between my teeth and bit it with the name Clothilde.

. . . I see Clothilde flouncing from my room in a pretence of fury, but coming back to say that the parliament had voted for the king to be dethroned and the royal family had been taken off to prison. It was where kings lived anyway, I told her. What was the palace but a prison? And Versailles, St James's, Windsor . . . I see an imperial eagle, cut down from a cathedral spire, being drawn in an open carriage through Paris, a chain round its neck and the red cap of liberty on its head. Beak and claws were chopped off and it was hung by the legs from an obelisk. That was nearly thirty years ago.

. . . I see, with eyes half shut, the men in this little London room. They have been retreating into frustration and disgust. They feel hemmed in by the law, poverty, society. A man's life isn't complete like this, and because he can't endure it unless it's fully lived he will exchange it for violent action. An act, however brutal, would be better than this claustrophobia. I believe I can help them if nobody else will: help them bring Paris to London.

*

Thistlewood stood apart, a tall man in a blue coat, velvet collar, blue trousers, distinct from the other men in the room. They kept away, hardly talking but standing and watching him. He had an effect on them and wouldn't lose it; wouldn't give away what he could see. He was gratified, hopeful, elated. Twelve had come to the tenement house in Fox Court tonight. Twelve good men and true. Or twelve apostles – he wasn't modest. It was better than he expected and next time there would be more. The thing was getting going at last, it would grow quickly now. He would avoid the old mistakes.

Brunt, a shoemaker, finished cramming newspaper into the window cracks. The black fringe that met his eyebrows, and the livid eyes, gave him a scowl which the best mood couldn't banish. Massive shoulders, thick neck, ferocious face – the name Brunt fitted him, he had invented it himself. It was easier to remember than other names he had used and nobody in the little room knew it wasn't his own.

Brunt went out to fetch a piece of red cotton, his wife's apron.

8

They had the front room on the second floor for themselves and their daughter, and this back one for shoemaking, which was let to Ings now. Brunt brought him to Fox Court this morning and told the landlady that he was a friend up from the country, looking for a lodging. The truth was, Brunt had met him for the first time in the White Hart yesterday. They were introduced by Edwards who could be useful that way: always ready to help a friend. The landlady agreed to let the back room to Ings and hoped he would be a good lodger. Brunt said he'd guarantee, but didn't tell her that Ings was a butcher out of work; she need never know. Ings had no money for the rent, so Brunt paid for him – a shilling a week. Again, it was Edwards who lent Brunt a pound in the pub. When Ings came back this evening he brought a wooden bed, his only furniture.

Brunt pushed the bed under the window and stood on it to hang up the red apron for a curtain. He could hardly reach but there were nails in the wood, he only had to spike the corners of the cotton. The skin of his fingers was scored and split like old leather that let the water in; with his stubby figure and ugly face they matched his name. He got off the bed: 'How's that?'

Edwards, lost in a huge brown coat, said, 'Keeps out the cold,' and tugged at his pale beard. 'Keeps the eyes out too.' He wore his hair to his shoulders and was the youngest in the room, no better dressed or washed than the others. They made approving noises, whistled through their teeth, rubbed their fingers. From the way their breath hung in the air they might be out in the cold night.

Brunt smoothed his hands down his shoemaker's apron: 'Little Ings, old friend, how's that? It's your room, you must make yourself at home. I told the lady your furniture would be along.' He laughed roughly: 'In a few days, I said.'

Ings, the butcher, laughed too. He was round and plump and friendly like a little bullock with frightened eyes, soon to be slaughtered. 'All I've got left is the bed,' he said. 'I sold everything and sent the money to my wife after she went back to Portsmouth where we came from.' He was talkative tonight, he would tell them the story. 'She took our three daughters and the son. I pawned my watch for the tickets – anywhere's better than bloody London. Soon as we got here things went wrong and never stopped. I had money when we came, that I saved from Portsmouth as a butcher. It all went. That was last summer –

9

the first of May, we came. I wish we never did. All they said about London you can throw away, worse than offal. Nine months is all it took and I got through everything.'

Brunt laughed again: 'In the White Hart like I first saw you, standing pints all round, playing cribbage.'

It made little Ings angry: 'I never went in there till my wife went back, not in the White Hart or any other pub. I never. My money didn't go like that. I got drunk three times in my life – that's nothing for a butcher.'

'I paid the rent for one month,' Brunt said, 'which ought to do. You wouldn't want it longer.' He looked at the tall man in the blue coat standing apart, hoping for assent, but Thistlewood seemed not to be listening: a puzzling figure screened from the rest, too proud or watchful to share his ambition easily.

Ings said, 'That's all I've got – the bloody bed. But it'll have to go and I'll send the money to Portsmouth.' His anger was already gone: nothing could crack his cheerfulness for long.

'I know a man who'd be interested,' Edwards said, his fingers reaching up to tug his beard. 'How much d'you want? I'll bring him next time.' There was something about Edwards: he could get things done, it was never too much trouble. Through him Ings had found a place to live.

'I'd take ten shillings.' Ings was grateful. 'Five shillings if it's a friend.'

'I'll fetch a chair,' Brunt said. 'And a bench – give me a hand, two of you.'

Each time the door was opened smoke backed down the chimney, gushing into the room. Little heat came from the fire, the coal was the poorest stuff. From the mantelpiece an oil lamp gave a yellow light that barely crossed the room. A few men kept their coats on, the rest didn't possess any.

Brunt put the chair near the fire: 'Mr Thistlewood!' and waved the tall man to it with a flourish. Performed by Brunt it was bizarre.

Thistlewood was the oldest of them, nearer fifty than forty: the only one who could be called Mister without irony, the officer among a squad of other ranks. Though far from smart or brisk he bore a shadow that was dimly military, a soldier's touch, as if he might once have commanded troops – long ago, for the army traces were faint. Since then, from looks, he hadn't had much luck. But among these men he carried authority, not just because they were younger. It was right that he should have the chair.

Three settled on the bench, three on the bed, the rest on the floor against the wall. Brunt said, 'Very cosy,' and laughed, then turned up the lamp and took a place at the end of the bench. 'Very revolutionary. The landlady should be pleased. Her house will be famous – where it all began. Twelve patriots with one chair between them, one lamp . . . '

'One idea,' Edwards said.

'There'll be pilgrimages here – a national shrine. My wife's apron will go in a museum.'

Quietly from the corner Davidson said, 'We could do with some decoration, some coloured bunting round the door.' He was a black man, the only one. His voice carried the balm of West Indian islands, not the rasp of London slums. 'I've got a big flag which my wife stitched a death's head on, for the elections.'

Harrison, on the bench, said, 'We brought back a tricolour from St Peter's Fields, the only one we saved – the army got the rest.' He was worse off than most, he hadn't had work since the year before last. Like others he had been in the army in the war and wore the tunic of his uniform. It helped keep his self-respect, but hadn't saved him from the cavalry charge against the crowd at Manchester last summer. 'The dead should have been buried in those flags like on a battlefield, but they never were. The flags were burnt, except the one we kept.'

Little Ings, on his bed beside Edwards, began to sing the Marseillaise, not knowing the words.

Brunt silenced him: 'You want to tell the landlady who we are? Have Sidmouth's men coming up the stairs?' He looked at Thistlewood, but the tall man on the chair pulled a silver snuff-box from his blue coat and took a pinch in silence. Brunt turned to Edwards: 'You're an artist? You could do us a picture for over the fireplace – something allegoric that nobody would understand.'

Edwards shifted on the bed: 'I'm a sculptor, that's not my style.' He sounded the best educated, apart from Thistlewood. Though his long hair and pale beard were dirty, his brown coat patched, his shoes in holes, he looked polished and refined against the others.

11

'You could do us a statue – a marble one of Liberty.'

Edwards tugged his beard. He wasn't a true sculptor, he had begun as a medical student but never got beyond anatomy. To earn money he worked for a surgeon, assisting at autopsies, laying out the dead, dissecting bodies for demonstration. From surgical casts and death masks he moved on to models of famous men made of plaster stolen from the hospital, which he sold in students' pubs. The most popular was his figure of Thomas Paine. It fired his idealism and trade was good cover for a revolutionary, but the nearest he got to sculpture was an order from a widow for her husband's tomb. He had an arrangement with the keeper of a mortuary and lost it when his politics came to light; then trudged the streets, trying to sell his models in private houses, lately with no success. His appearance belied the record – he got by, somehow. There were ways a young man with wits could live, and poverty was a great destroyer of ideals, even scruples, which vanished at the prospect of a meal.

'At home we'd have music,' Davidson, the black man, said. 'Flute and drum and a woman singing.' And the wind in the sugar cane and fireflies signalling in the night. Davidson had come far from Jamaica. Though young, he had the battered look of a man who had exchanged one slavery for another. But he had a right here because Jamaica belonged to the empire, which gave him a claim. And what had happened? He appealed to the men in the room: 'You said it, little Ings – London's no good, nobody's ever done a thing for me. All those years I never made a friend, not one.' He spoke without sadness. Resentment had melted into acquiescence. He had learnt to keep quiet and hope for better days.

Cooper, next to Harrison on the bench, said, 'Any amount of blacks where I live in Limehouse.' He had been a sailor, he still wore his canvas jumper and wide trousers tied with a lanyard and a black silk rag round his collar.

'I don't go with them,' Davidson said, 'though I'm one myself. I've found them very ignorant.'

Harrison said, 'What d'you expect?'

'I'm not complaining,' the black man said. 'It's just I never made a friend. When I first came I studied to be a lawyer, three years in an office, but the boss was prejudiced, that's all you can say. Man, I tell you, when you're up against that, you just turn away and try another place. So I was apprentice to a cabinet-maker. I did a good job, good with my hands and learning well, but it was the same – prejudice.'

'You can't blame them,' Harrison said, 'when there isn't work for the English.'

Cooper, the sailor, said, 'I've seen them in their own country – Africa, the Indies, anywhere. Some are good, some aren't. Like in Limehouse. You get to know. I'll call a man my friend and he's black or brown or yellow . . .' But he stopped, having said too much. A man doesn't become a sailor to sit and talk.

'It was a girl I came unstuck over,' Davidson said. 'Or her father, I ought to say. He shot me when he found what his baby girl and I were doing.' He laughed softly at the memory: 'Would you let your daughter marry a black man?' and didn't wait to hear the answer: 'The mother was the same but you can work on a woman, which you can't with a man. She winked at us, the way I thought she might fancy it herself, but the father went crazy when he knew. The girl was sixteen and juicy, just juicy. Squeeze her and it came out everywhere, eyes, tongue, tits, between the legs, she couldn't stop. So he lay in wait with his gun. The bullet went through my hat – some shooting! He tried to get me for rape. Rape! – man, I tell you, that little girl couldn't have too much, she was mad for everything in my possession.' Crossed-legged on the floor Davidson took a handful of his grubby trousers at the crutch and eased himself. 'I'll say this for the police – they weren't convinced, they pulled him in for shooting me. He sang like a chicken, he said I could have her if I promised not to prosecute. So I promised. Then he made me wait till she was twenty-one, so I promised. So who was the gentleman? He sent her to Scotland and she was married to a little cock the same colour as herself, I heard. I was so mad, I swallowed poison. It was the mother that saved me. Why she bothered or what she wanted out of me . . . Soon as I was well she saw me off – that's what started it. Last job I had, I got thirty shillings a week. It's prejudice, nothing else. I never made a friend in England.'

Brunt said, 'You've got plenty now, all of us in this room.'

'Thirty shillings!' Ings cried. 'I never got that as butcher after I came to London. A pound was best, when I had my shop in Smithfield. No luck, that's what.'

'A pound's good,' Brunt said.

Ings was too excited to stop: 'I had my shop three months –
all last summer. I put everything in it. But the summer being
hot was against me. Meat – you know what it is. If I'd lasted till
winter I'd have come through. So I had to sell. Then I started a
coffee stall. One trouble was, I didn't know the job, it wasn't
like a butcher's. It never brought in the custom. The money all
going, I didn't know what to do. My wife went back – I don't
have it against her, she's a knowing woman. That's when I met
Edwards.' Ings winked at the young man with the beard. 'He
came to the coffee stall with his pamphlets.'

'Ings sold them over the counter for me,' Edwards said.

'For twopence of gin,' Ings said, 'and a steak when I hadn't
eaten. Or I don't know what I'd have done to keep going.
Without Edwards I'd never be here. He saved me for a bit.
Even so, I watched the stall go down like the shop. In the end I
had to sell, but I got nothing, it was robbery – all I did was
stand and watch while they settled the price as if it wasn't mine,
it was theirs to buy and sell. They're smart in London. After
that it was the furniture, except the bed, so I could send money
to my wife. She needed it, with the kids in Portsmouth. I went
back to Smithfield to try if I could get a job. I'm a butcher, I
know the work, but when they saw I was from the country they
looked at me as if I wasn't there, I was an empty space in front
of them, a hole in the air they could see through, not a butcher
standing up and asking for a job. Knowing nobody, was the
reason. Like Davidson says, a man needs friends or else . . . '
Between his fingers he flicked a matchstick into the fire.

They were waiting for Thistlewood. Every few minutes,
delicately like a ritual, he took a pinch from his silver snuff-box.
Watching the others: a thin man with slow brown eyes in a
sallow face. Sometimes he shut them to look at things in distant
places, years ago. Large drooping nose, arched eyebrows,
brushed whiskers: not handsome, not quite ugly, but marked
with a sullen melancholy influence. His lips moved as if trying
out the words to use, practising in silence.

'A shoemaker could earn two or three pounds with luck,'
Brunt said, 'but nobody wants shoes now, they haven't the
money. Anyone can tell you, who's in the trade. Am I right,
Tidd?' He turned to a man who hadn't spoken, another
shoemaker with a mild soft face and bald head shining in the
lamplight. Apart from Thistlewood he alone could be over

forty, though in the dimness some of the others looked prematurely worn.

'You've only to look about you,' Tidd said. He was shy and meek, unused to speaking, only at ease at his shoemaker's bench. A blush rose into his bald head at the sound of his voice.

Brunt repeated loudly, 'Look about you and what d'you see? Men in parliament who argue how they can plunder the country. For a year I've been down to ten shillings. Lucky I was in the war with the Duke of Wellington. When I was paid off I gave the bounty to my wife and now it's gone, and the Duke's in the cabinet and thinks ten shillings is what his soldiers fought for.'

Harrison, the soldier who had been at St Peter's Fields, said, 'Mind you, I can mention advantages in the army.'

'Join it often and don't stay long,' Brunt agreed. 'In the war there were enough regiments for that. Enlist in one, take the bounty, then desert and when the money's gone you join the next.' He laughed and said, 'Another thing' – nodding towards the front room – 'it's telling on the wife and daughter.' There was menace in his voice, he couldn't help it. He threw his scowl round the men's faces as if challenging them to wonder how the uncouth Brunt could love a woman, or she love him.

Thistlewood was ready to speak. Somehow they knew it and stopped talking. Slowly he looked round the room, surveying the men who had come: blunt, solid, simple men, not like the clever French ones, but they would do, there was nobody else. One or two were old friends, a few he had met recently, some were new tonight. But he was leader, they would look up to him. He could show them how these things were done, from his experience. The shoemaker Brunt, though coarse and perhaps stupid, would be one of the strongest. Edwards, the long-haired artist, had proved himself by bringing others and promised more. Ings, the butcher, and Tidd, the other shoemaker, would be forced by poverty to keep faith, and Davidson as a black man was welcome. Harrison and Cooper, soldier and sailor, probably had more idea of the work than the rest together. And there were men who hadn't spoken – Gilchrist, Strange, Wilson – or whose names Thistlewood didn't know, who had come tonight out of hope, despair, curiosity, even the same elation that drove himself. He took one more pinch of snuff, snapped the silver box shut, and said, 'Where's Bradburn?'

15

'Bradburn?' Brunt looked round, indignant that anyone was missing. 'Didn't he come?'

'He took the money,' Davidson said. 'We won't see him again, he's not a fool, not Bradburn.'

'Imprisoned without trial,' Edwards said, 'like all good men.'

Thistlewood said, 'I got twenty-four pike sticks from the country. I wrote to Lincolnshire and they were sent.' He was born a Lincoln man and there were people up there who might not be pleased to see him back; others who had nothing to forgive him for, who could still be useful. 'Straight green wood and very strong – I gave them to Bradburn to have iron points put on. He said he had a friend.'

'You should have let me have them,' Edwards said. 'I know a man who'd do it, no questions asked.' Edwards could be relied on. He would always find someone to get a job done, cheaper than most.

'Bradburn took them away,' Davidson said. 'I watched him. The money too – man, I tell you, you won't see him again.' The black man wasn't bitter, he just knew about people.

'I don't care for Bradburn, he can hang himself,' Thistlewood said, 'but it's the pike sticks and the money.' He fell back into silence, he would let the men talk, to find out their ideas. There was plenty of time. The road to Fox Court had taken years. He had learnt to be cautious, he must control this ferment or they would be in trouble. Since Paris, as an English revolutionary, he had seen what might be done. A transparent gauze dropped over his eyes. They swam over deep layers of time, touching small points of recollection.

*

. . . I see Robespierre in his seat on the benches. A lawyer from Arras, not many years older than myself – another young man from the north. At first he seemed ineffectual, a lightweight among so many heavies. Slight, ascetic, nimble with the movements of a cat. He wore glasses which sometimes he took off to look around. His eyes searched the tumult for a theme, tracking down the future in the chaos of the present. It must be here somewhere, like oxygen in the air, if only he could isolate it. His pasty upturned nose probed for signs. The future was close at hand, he simply had to find it.

I watched him for two years, sensing that he was the man to follow. A lifetime later I still believe that of them all he was the one with a touch of greatness, who never deserved the evil they said of him. The men who maligned him were midgets vilifying him for their own cheap popularity, like the pimps they were.

The revolution didn't take up all my days. I lounged in cafés or the Hôtel de Moscovie, reading and talking – the life of a student in Paris. But often I went to the debates and it was Robespierre I looked for. Biting his nails, twitching his shoulders, sulking or pondering higher things, unaware of the clamour round him, alone in the crowd. Nervous but self-important, poor but dandyish, still young yet old before his time, mercurial and humourless and strict. He wasn't a lovable man, he was too austere and vain, hardly a complete man at all but a speaking instrument that must be played. When the president called him he went quickly to the tribune, brusque and unsmiling. His voice was strident, sometimes stuttering, the voice of a small man with a giant task, but he used it like a sword. His enemies feared his deadly seriousness – a man of absolutes, believing in everything he said, as he would in a theorem of mathematics. His heavenly city was a place for the world's victims, for Jews and paupers and blacks – no wonder the gallery drank his words. When he stepped down they shouted for more. He was worshipped for being modest, thrifty, obscure even in his triumph. Women swooned. I saw a housewife follow him back to his seat with a handkerchief and wipe the sweat off his face. I thought of Jesus – I believe he did too. When I told Clothilde she said, 'Ah, that Robespierre . . .' and sighed. He could get all the women he wanted, if he wanted.

I had an instinct that my career was locked to his. My two years in Paris were dominated by that passionate unswerving figure. I learnt his speeches by heart for my own use later, but couldn't claim his genius or the luck to be flung like him into a revolution that was in full swing. I might copy him, no more, and hope for his courage.

. . . I see his room in the Rue St Honoré where I tried to get to know him better. It was furnished for a puritan with a single bed, small desk, bookcase, some common chairs. The curtains were made by his landlady from her old dresses – I thought of that when I watched Brunt pin his wife's apron over the window at Fox Court. But Robespierre wasn't easy to know, he didn't want friends, he could hardly shake hands without distaste. He was obsessed with intrigue and treachery, convinced that agents were sent to persecute or murder him. He wasn't a man for compromise, the reply to the assassin's knife was the guillotine – fear answered by superior fear. I took him a gift of oranges when I heard they were his favourite fruit and helped his chronic constipation, but it made him more suspicious. I didn't know that a kitchen knife was found in a basket of oranges brought by a woman to his door.

. . . I see his face close to. Yellow and pitted with smallpox below the curled brown hair or powdered wig. A woman's face, too soft for a man. The famous bilious colour of his cheeks came from greenish veins under the surface of the cheeks, giving him an unchanging look. But there was nothing static about his eyes. They were green or fawn or blue according to the occasion and the light – the light inside. Shy or shifty or imperious or angry. Dull one moment, fiery the next, then clouded again by asthma. The eyes of a sick, paranoid, disagreeable man with the glint of a machine driven to breaking point, a spirit stretched to the limit by the immense power of its rectitude.

. . . I see the look in Lord Sidmouth's eyes, that brief moment when they fixed me from the Speaker's chair. They too contained a moral certainty, a cold and hard and gleaming confidence in their righteousness. That frozen look has followed me for thirty years.

*

The door of the little room opened and another man came in; stood blinking with one eye for a moment, uncertain if he had the right address: 'Fox Court, is it?' A thin man with a crooked face. Only the left eye blinked. One side was normal, but his jaw was grotesquely twisted and the right eye had sunk into his skull, deep between the brow and cheekbone. It lay abandoned in its hole, useless.

Brunt said, 'Come in, come in, old friend,' and to Thistlewood in the chair: 'This is Adams, the one I told you of, a member of the profession – that makes three of us.' He winked at Tidd, the second shoemaker. The stranger hesitated in the doorway. 'Adams was a soldier like the best of us,' Brunt said. 'We met in France – Cambrai, wasn't it?' He searched his friend's single good eye, trying to remember what name Adams had known him by or which regiment he was in. Guessing, he said, 'The Life Guards, as I remember.'

Adams corrected him: 'The Blues,' and frowned with half his face.

'The Blues it was.'

The anxiety was mutual. Like Brunt, Adams had been only a cobbler for the army, mending soldiers' boots. Once he had made a pair of riding boots for a colonel. Like others he found a more dubious livelihood. Now the two campaigners' memories had turned heroic, they didn't care to be reminded of the inglorious truth. Adams said, 'I did seven years in the army.'

'Can you use a sword?' Thistlewood asked.

'I used to.' Adams stood stiffly in the door.

'A gun?'

'Years ago, but I've had no practice.' Adams clenched his thin fists: 'But I can defend myself and attack – I was good in those days, it hasn't gone.' He put on a fierce look, affecting only the left side of his face; the right stayed dead.

'Where d'you live?'

'Hole-in-the-wall Passage, by Brooke's Market. Lately I've been inside.' Quickly Adams added, 'The debtors' house for a month – I got out this morning.'

'Caught him on his way from prison,' Brunt told them. 'We can't have too many shoemakers.'

Softly Tidd, the older shoemaker, said, 'Coming here's the best way back to prison. Next time it'll be Newgate.' But the prospect was too terrifying and he was sorry he had spoken. He could define their fate by putting it into words. They couldn't risk such folly, there would be no danger if he hadn't uttered it. He gulped to swallow his terror and waited for the blush to fade from his bald head.

Thistlewood smiled. He was the last to reject a man for having been in prison, but wished it was for a better crime – sedition would do. With the merest nod he showed that the recruit was enrolled. Adams shut the door, stumbled over men's legs and picked a corner of the floor by Davidson, the black. Even his good eye was shortsighted, but the fierce look stayed on half his crooked face, to keep his soldier's reputation.

Edwards, the artist, tugged his beard nervously. Tidd shrank into his coat, hoping not to be asked to say more: diffidence was his element. Ings' wary little eyes darted in his butcher's face. The fire hissed coldly, the flame of the lamp drooped through the greasy glass, a chilling vacuity crept round the room. The men's shadows hung like demons on the wall, waiting for Thistlewood.

At last he spoke: 'Friends . . . ' It wasn't right. Next time he would try 'citizens'. Before he got further there was a tread on the stairs and the door opened again.

Brunt said, 'Bradburn – here he is.'

'I thought you'd taken off,' Davidson said. 'Man, you had the money.'

Bradburn came in with a bundle of pikes, put them on the floor, pulled some out and passed them round; then sat on the bundle. The men tried them for weight and spring. They were cut from new green wood, taller than a man.

Thistlewood examined one of the crude iron points: just a flat blade nailed on, not what he had asked for. He shouldn't have trusted Bradburn with the job, he should have got Edwards. But it would do, it was a beginning: soon they would have swords, muskets, grenades, artillery. He gripped the pike and struck it on the floor. It sounded defiant and brave. A pike was democratic, symbolic, better than a gun: 'This is the people's weapon, everyone will have one. It was good enough for the citizens of Paris . . . ' He struck the floor again.

Brunt told the others, 'Mr Thistlewood was in the revolution,' and cocked a thumb towards him. The men muttered in admiration.

Thistlewood saw that Brunt was a sort of adjutant. Tidd, the second oldest, would be sergeant if he could overcome his shyness. Harrison and Adams and any who had been in the army would take charge of weapon training, and Cooper, the sailor, might know about artillery. Thistlewood looked round the rest: not promising, but much could be done. With an ideal and a hope they could be raised from the lowest level, lifted more easily for having so far to rise. Men could surprise themselves, he had seen it. A commander was all they needed. But he shouldn't think in military terms, it was a political revolution, though armed. And he would need a secretary. Edwards would do, he would have good handwriting. Thistlewood looked at him, thankful for his youth and energy. Edwards held a pike too, as if uncertain how it might behave:

this vicious thing, to be pushed into a living body.

'What's the plan?' Edwards asked, putting the weapon down. 'When do we begin?'

'I can't hold out much longer,' Ings said. 'I haven't a penny left and not likely to find one. I promised to send more to Portsmouth, but after the bed's gone . . . '

It released the others.

'One week's all I can wait.'

'They don't know what being poor is.'

'They don't know the state the country's in, the bastards.'

'It'll be the end of them, it's got to come.'

'Like Judgment Day.'

'Can't come too quick.'

'One pound a week! – what d'you do with a pound?'

'Spend it in the White Hart.'

'Mind you, what d'you expect from that lot?'

'Listen man, they can't escape, it's up to us, it's the only way.'

Thistlewood struck the pike on the floor again. He must fit their impatience to a plan but not have it wrecked by haste. He wasn't sure who to trust, he only knew the danger. He said, 'You remember Judas?' and glowered at their dingy startled faces.

They cast uneasy eyes around or stared at nothing. Davidson hitched his trousers again, Cooper tucked one leg under the other, Bradburn shifted on the pile of pikes, Tidd blushed helplessly, Edwards stopped tugging his beard to pick his fingernails. The lamp was smoking and Brunt got up to turn it down. Adams rubbed his single eye.

Davidson spoke; ran his fingers through the mat of crinkled hair, chasing some distant childhood scene or the echo of an old Jamaican tale, and said like a prophet, 'Better for that man if he'd never been born – that's my conclusion and I speak as one who taught in Sunday school.' It was a time of his life which ended in disgrace, which he wouldn't share with these men till he knew them better, but he could slip back into his preacher's tone.

'The man who splits,' Brunt announced, 'Christ Allfucking-mighty, I'll cut his throat.'

Adams, stiffly through the side of his mouth that wasn't dead, said, 'Spies are the worst buggers.'

'That was your trouble last time, Mr Thistlewood,' Edwards said, as a statement or a question.

A private smile flickered like something in code on Thistlewood's face. He wouldn't talk about the past, he asked nothing about these men's lives and expected the same from them. A hint of his career, an allusion to some event, a name dropped, were all he needed. He said, 'Spies are the minister's favourite weapon.'

Ings said brightly, 'Lord Sidmouth – that one?'

'Typical of the man.'

'You know him?'

'We've been in touch.'

Edwards, who knew more than the others, said, 'You fought a duel.'

'I challenged him but he was frightened, we never met.' Thistlewood's name as a swordsman was notorious in Whitehall. He gripped the pike: 'He knew I'd kill him – that was some satisfaction.'

'Good for you, Mr Thistlewood,' Ings said, and rubbed his hands.

'He couldn't forgive me, he got me for a breach of peace.'

Adams asked, 'Prison?' He had come out of it today. But Thistlewood didn't answer, he had given away more than he meant.

Edwards said, 'You've got it in for him.' Then laughed: 'Who wouldn't? – for an old man who gets his pleasure from suspending habeas corpus.'

'It's his turn to be suspended.' The gentle negro voice from the corner. 'From the top of St Paul's Cathedral by his balls.'

'Lord Sidmouth takes the prize among that lot,' Ings said. 'Like a rabbit galantine, is what I say – mostly jelly. What meat there is, it's got no colour, no blood in it.'

Harrison said, 'Blood on his hands – anyone can tell you, who was at St Peter's Fields. That was Sidmouth's doing. He said they used the flat of their swords. Ask the fifteen who got killed if it was the flats. I never been so frightened, and I went through the war. It's a wonder it wasn't fifteen hundred – trampled by the horses mostly.'

'You learn what to expect,' Brunt said, 'and keep away.'

Ings said, 'Open your mouth and they shove something in – brick, spade, boot, anything they've got.'

The rest joined in.

'Not just Sidmouth.'

'The whole cabinet.'

'The prime minister, Lord Castlereagh, the Duke . . . '

'From the top down it's the system, not the parties, there's nothing to choose, right or left, lords or shopkeepers.'

'What I've always said, shopkeepers are as bad as anyone.'

'Priests the same.'

'Bishops the worst.'

'What they hear in Whitehall or Westminster or the places they live in – they'll never find out.'

'Too proud to go among the people and ask.'

'Too fucking frightened.' Brunt swore most but he had only one word.

'Anything they get told comes from men who've got an interest.'

'Who it pays to hide the truth.'

'Or twist it for themselves.'

'Man, I tell you, the people are ignorant just the same.'

'People don't know what the fuck's going on.'

'Except a lot of men are making money.'

'Going abroad.'

'Getting bigger houses.'

'More horses, carriages . . . '

'Finding where the profit is.'

Tidd screwed himself up to speak: 'The people have been dead for years,' and slipped back into silence behind a deepening blush.

'Dead for years, you've said it, Tidd – the people stopped and we went ahead, we left them behind.'

'So what the fuck are we doing?'

'A direct act, that's what.'

'It's for us to settle what we can do.'

'A black man's against it all the time, man, I tell you.'

'I know the feeling,' Edwards said. 'You're on your own, angry inside, looking for a way.'

'Listen, man . . . '

Thistlewood listened. They must feel participators. It was a matter of timing, to catch the emotion for each step. The men would be the performers, he only had to chivvy, stimulate them with his vision. For years he had made speeches in pub

23

parlours, at revolutionary societies, in dusty halls, on wagons dragged into the crowd; his eloquence was famous. Tonight was no occasion for that. For the first time he saw the possibility: they could change things, they could make a difference. He said, 'I'm thinking of the day when all the shops are shut, plundered by the people.'

'Not the butchers.'

'The churches too,' Thistlewood said.

'You'il never do it – not a chance.'

Edwards said, 'What we need is to make them jump.'

'Grab them in the balls.' With big black hands Davidson clutched his trousers again for reassurance.

'Especially Sidmouth's.'

'His dropped off.'

'Blow up something.'

'Blow up the fucking lot.'

'Blow up the machine, stop it spinning money for them'

'Power and privileges for their families, father to son for ever.'

'It's a good machine if you've got a share.'

Thistlewood said, 'But it needs men to work it – it burns them like fuel.' When he spoke the others stopped. 'There's no shortage of fuel. It's everywhere for the picking, in the streets and villages and new towns, going cheap. But it's explosive.' He had set the men going, he need only watch and keep them in control.

'One spark to touch it off.'

'Strike the match and the people join, they're waiting.'

'Set fire to the barracks.'

'You've forgotten the army.'

'Fuck the army, it's only men the same as us.'

'If I know soldiers, they're frightened.'

'When London's risen they'll never attack their own people.'

'At St Peter's Fields they did.'

'You've forgotten the cabinet – they've got the officers and arsenals.'

'They'll know nothing till there's a people's government and we'll have it ready.'

'Send to Dover, Southampton . . .'

'Nobody can leave without a people's passport.'

'You'd never do it without arms.'

24

'We'll make them, we'll get the stuff – an ammunition factory in this house.'

'One big swipe like killing the king.'

'The prime minister's better.'

'Chop the lot.'

'What I've always said, if there's one minister left alive you can march to Whitehall and ask to be fucking hanged.'

Brunt let out a dying gargle and hung his head limply to one side, his tongue out. Some men laughed, but Tidd turned white with horror, the blush draining from his bald head. Since being taken as a boy to an execution he had felt the blindfold, the rough hemp whiskers under his ears, the last seconds to the drop, not knowing how many were left. Hundreds of times, by day or night, he had fallen like that man into the dark. He caught his breath in a convulsion, clutched his throat and began to say something – anything would do.

Someone else got there first.

'Kill them all, the whole cabinet.'

'Corner them like rats and go in with our shirtsleeves up.'

'I've got my butcher's knife, I can get an edge on that.'

Edwards jumped up from the bed: 'You see this book – an ordinary book,' holding it up and tapping it. 'There's nothing to say you can't carry a book in your hand, nobody would stop you. You walk into parliament with it . . . ' With a snap like a conjurer he flicked it open: it was an iron box.

'For fuck's sake.'

'I had it made – a friend of mine. And sawn-off gun barrels – he'll get them cheap. Fill a tube with powder and plug the ends with lead and put a touch hole in it for a piece of fuse and hide it in your book, all innocence, nothing wrong, and go up in the gallery when the house is full and the ministers are on the bench down there . . . ' Edwards' eyes described the lethal work and he laughed.

He was irrepressible. Thistlewood had come to love this fiery young man, and needed him. Edwards' name reached him long before they met, when Thistlewood was in prison after challenging Lord Sidmouth to a duel. From his guards he heard of a student who was going from pub to pub, drumming up support against the government, getting known for his reckless plots – hare-brained ideas that never got beyond the madcap moment of their invention. But Thistlewood was attracted, and

25

after leaving prison he found that Edwards too had hoped to work together. The mature revolutionary, seasoned in campaigns and prisons, was flattered and encouraged by the young rebel, lit with imagination and not soured by disappointment.

The men were suspicious of Edwards' plan.

'You'd never get in, I went down there once.'

'They don't let us vote for them, why should they let us watch?'

'The cabinet's all we want – they meet in Downing Street every day, fourteen of them.'

'Break in and cut them down.'

'With my butcher's knife.'

'They change the time, you'd have to know.'

'They have a cabinet dinner every week.'

'They stopped, it was in the paper, they haven't had a dinner since Christmas.'

'They stopped fucking eating, they aren't human, they can go for months without.'

Thistlewood was heartened by this: impatient, dangerous, violent at last. He had watched it before and this was a good beginning. Great events were at hand, the people were seething. Too often he had been promised support but let down. These men, without experience or resources, wouldn't fail. He mustn't fail them, and stood up: 'That means more men. Three for each minister. Next time every man brings two more. And swords, pistols, anything . . . '

'Twelve shillings for a pair of pistols.' Edwards put the false book under his coat. 'Four shillings for an army one, from the war.'

'Who's got four shillings?'

Bradburn picked up the bundle of pikes: 'Where's the magazine?'

Brunt opened a cupboard by the chimney: 'Little Ings, we'll use this till your things arrive.' He gave his short rough laugh; stacked the pikes in the cupboard and shut the door. 'What about supper?'

Some hadn't had a meal for days. They looked at Thistlewood. Perhaps he was hungry too and would celebrate with them: the birth of a revolution. But a man with his record would be watched by Sidmouth's men.

Edwards saw his hesitation: 'There's the White Hart where Brunt and Ings were last night. I know the landlord, he'd give us a room at the back.'

'There's a policeman lives opposite, from Bow Street,' Brunt said. 'He'll see there's something on.'

'We could send there for food and have it brought back,' Edwards said. 'Here's a shilling.'

Thistlewood gave another. Others shook their clothes to see what fell out. Some didn't move and Ings dropped a little sob, then converted it to a giggle. Brunt said, 'Nobody got any more? I'm the same, for fuck's sake, I can't get work to earn any but I've still got a pound.' He fetched it, also a copper jug: 'Get some beer and a pint of gin if there's enough.'

Edwards patted his pocket: 'I'll see to it.'

'I'll come with you,' Davidson offered.

From her window Mrs Brunt watched a black man with shabby trousers and no socks, and a pale young man in a huge coat with her jug, go down the steps and out of Fox Court towards Holborn. It was cold enough to snow, she thought.

Up in the back room the men waited, seldom talking. Brunt tried to stir life into the fire, Tidd blew on his fingers to thaw them. The cupboard door creaked and the men watched it swing open to show the bundle of iron-tipped pikes. From his bed Ings kicked it shut. Thistlewood smiled. It was a cold bare little room, hardly worthy of the night.

*

A clerk came into Lord Sidmouth's office and with the least nod to the huge mahogany desk went to the fireplace; knelt on the hearthrug to push a poker through the bars. With tongs he picked coal from the scuttle and placed it on the fire. The flame turned to smoke, a sour new smell joined the winter morning and drifted into the room. This show of life was an insult to literature and to the minister: he closed the leather volume, put it in his desk, pushed the drawer shut. The interruption caught him halfway through one of the pages of his life.

It had been his favourite pleasure since Lady Sidmouth died ten years ago. His heir had gone mad, his younger son was devoid of talent, his daughters had brought him the four dullest sons-in-law a man could have, but to console him on the first Christmas of his grief his children gave him a journal embossed with the Sidmouth arms, a gift to brighten widowhood. Scrupulously he copied his loneliness into the blank pages and each Christmas received another volume. The old ones were locked in his desk, a treasure to count across the years, and there was hardly an entry that he didn't know by heart. The first was the most poignant: '*Last year it pleased a gracious God to take to Himself as pure a spirit as ever animated a perishable frame, but for her sorrowing husband the soul of all worldly happiness was gone and he could only pray for that tranquillity of mind which might fit him for real duties.*'

It set the tone for the thoughts on his career which he phrased in solemn hymns to the honour of his wife. One day these flights of art would be trapped in print, though not before his death: modesty was one of the minister's most admired possessions. But whoever wrote his biography would have the journal. Sidmouth would never see the published book, he would be united with his wife by then, but if anyone deserved a foretaste it was the hero – and perhaps the heroine. By reciting passages aloud in the words that would carry them into history he was testifying to his life; to his marriage too.

From the desk he watched the clerk impatiently; surveyed the empty chairs and bleak proportions of his office. A mist crept from Whitehall through the tall windows, rolled across the carpet, lapped the furniture, climbed the grey walls to the corners of the ceiling. The glint of a polished table, a gilt picture frame, an inkstand, a silver bell, appeared like beacons on a distant shore. All his widowed years he had worked in this room: years of most significance in his life. It said something for celibacy that till his wife died he hadn't found his true powers as a politician. Though he had been Speaker of parliament, lord President of the Council, even Prime Minister for two dim years, those portfolios were forgotten. A rare memory of his prime ministership was when Nelson told him that he prayed for it to be the most glorious in history; in his greater wisdom God had ignored the prayer.

The clerk at the fireplace was insufferable. Sidmouth got up, went to one of the windows, stood looking down into the street. Snow muffled the traffic. There must be ice on the pavement, from the way a policeman placed his boots, and Sidmouth remembered the accident this morning on the way from his home in Richmond Park. A coal wagon had skidded on Putney

Hill, the driver couldn't stop it. It struck the gutter and turned over, spilling sacks across the snow. In a moment, as the minister's carriage drove past, a woman and two men began picking up the coal. They were safe, they had time to fill their bags and pockets before the police were called. But it made Sidmouth boil: these scavengers looting under his eyes. He lowered the window and shouted. The woman, a lump of coal in her hand, looked up and from a mask of terror and misery fixed him with her eyes; then gave a shriek of animal laughter like something in a farmyard and threw the lump. It missed his face but came through the window. The coachman didn't stop, they drove to Whitehall with the coal on the floor.

There was too much of that sort of thing, but in the suburbs Sidmouth was spared the worst. Thank God he had accepted a house in Richmond Park from the king. Reviewing such landmarks the voice of the biographer, rehearsed and memorised, spoke: '*The king offered him the Duchy of Lancaster and an earldom and a life pension and the Garter twice, but he declined them all. Nobody more disinterested, more free from ambition or avarice, existed. The king said, "You are a proud man but so am I. Why should I allow you to ruin your family, why should I sleep uneasy on my pillow because you won't comply?" In the end, guided by duty and devotion to his majesty, he accepted the house.*' Out at Richmond he could walk anywhere without being recognised.

Very different here in London, especially since the trouble up in Manchester last summer: Peterloo, it was now called, to mock the Duke of Wellington's great victory. Only fifteen were killed when unarmed civilians had to be dispersed by cavalry, and one was a policeman trampled by the horses, but the effects had drifted south. When Sidmouth walked with Lord Castlereagh up Whitehall they were followed by a booing, mocking crowd: a nasty occasion, not because Sidmouth was frightened for himself – he was incapable of that – but because it showed the eternal stupidity of the lower class. Castlereagh tried to make a joke of it: 'Here we go, two ministers of the cabinet, the most popular men in England, through a grateful and admiring crowd.' Sidmouth was ashamed to be seen with him in public. From the rumours, half the cabinet lived in a brothel, even the Duke, and Castlereagh was the worst: picking up women by the Serpentine according to the common story. Looking down into the wintry street, remembering those jeers, Sidmouth shivered.

Thank God he had never been guilty of despair. But the truth was, there were savages in England.

He listened for the clerk to put down the tongs, sweep the ashes and leave the room; then returned slowly to his desk. Before writing the best passages in his journal he liked to speak them aloud; to expand, posture, orate, modelling himself on Burke whom he had watched as a young member of parliament. He had been a pallbearer at Burke's funeral: he had the copyright to his style.

Hands behind him and feet apart, he rocked forwards on his toes – a trick of Burke's, but Burke's shoes never squeaked – and spoke to the sombre paintings, the king's portrait and bust of Burke, the upholstered chairs and future readers of his biography. His voice was light, clear, fresh for an elderly man who had once held the highest elected office, ringing through the big room with conviction, not imagination; slicing, rather than resounding: '*He could challenge anyone to question the purity of his motives. His loyalty and patriotism were undeviating. His rectitude never failed. Self-interest had no influence on his actions. No man more cheerfully sacrificed personal feelings to his duty. He may not always have been popular or appreciated, but he believed*' – he raised his eyes to the ceiling and beyond – '*he prayed that he would be remembered. After thirty-six years in parliament he was at the height of his potential, straining to complete the work entrusted to him.*' He paused for his shoes to squeak. '*Hard criticism was one thing to bear, an evil conscience quite another, and with God's help he never suffered from that. Sometimes it saddened him that in the cabinet his measures were not supported as he would have liked, but he knew that each step, however stern, was approved by the supreme authority of England. And in that approval, bestowed by a king noted for his piety, he felt the touch of God's favour. Since his wife's lamented death it was his finest inspiration.*'

Enough. It wouldn't do to be found by Hobhouse in mid-speech. Yet he wasn't sure: he was never at his best in public and would be sorry if these solos – the timely shrug and warning finger, the slap of palm on mahogany, even the squeak of leather – were lost. Sometimes he was tempted to arrange for the secretary to come in by chance and catch a performance for the sake of history. Diffidence prevailed. He took the journal from its drawer and for an instant was disappointed that the new paragraph hadn't written itself, but gravely transcribed it on the empty page; slid the book away, took out his watch and compared it with the Doric temple-clock on the mantelpiece – a sixtieth birthday present from his family; picked up the silver bell and rang it sharply once.

'Well, Hobhouse,' he said when the secretary was seated beyond the desk. Sidmouth wouldn't waste time on the snowy morning or the accident on Putney Hill: 'Our friends – what news have we today?'

Hobhouse was twenty years younger than his minister, with a papery face, long pale hands, legs twisting round each other. He opened a file of documents and folded his arms: 'They meet more often now – nearly every day.'

'Nearly every day . . . ' Years of deliberation had given Sidmouth the habit of repeating another man's words while thinking of his own.

With care the secretary uncurled his fingers and let them run among his papers: 'They're becoming impatient, they're desperate to get on with it.' The same couldn't be said of Hobhouse. His movements and drawling voice were in no hurry. Like a snake it seemed just possible, but unlikely, that he would strike.

'Get on with what, Hobhouse?'

'The West End job, they call it.'

'The West End job . . . ' Sidmouth stood up and walked slowly to the window again. London looked secure enough, smothered under snow, wrapped up and safe. Hard to believe that the population was now a million; to remember the terraces and squares and chains of selfsame houses that since the war had rolled out over farms and gardens and old estates; to think of the faceless new towns in the north, the mills, mines, factories which had brought such wealth and disaffection. From his window the view was comfortably unchangeable, it could be any winter morning of the last fifty years. Yet there were men down there who wanted to break the rules, crack the timeless pattern. 'The West End job,' he repeated, watching his breath on the cold glass. 'What kind of a job is that?'

'They're vague, they have no plan.'

'That is dangerous, Hobhouse – an unformed plot is the most elusive kind. We must help them. Give them an idea, encourage them – it's what they need.' The minister's voice rose higher, more ethereal as his thoughts moved over precedents and possibilities, back across the years and on into the future. 'It's something we have learnt, have we not? – to turn the other man's opportunity into our own.'

Hobhouse allowed himself a smile: 'York, you mean?'

'York, I mean.'It was one of Sidmouth's first duties at the ministry, when the Luddites were terrorising factory owners and breaking machinery. A judge at the assizes, by his mistaken leniency, had shown the need for an example and the new minister didn't flinch. He sent Hobhouse north to investigate the cases against prisoners awaiting trial and hasten any likely to end in a conviction. The secretary justified his confidence and seventeen were hanged at York Castle, which promised well; the following year was remembered for the peace enjoyed by England, though there had been other calls for retribution: 'York, yes – also Chester and Lancaster . . . '

Hobhouse sensed the mood: 'Between them, twenty-three were hanged.'

'And Ely . . . '

'Five at Ely.'

'Leicester . . . '

'Six.'

'Derby . . . '

'Three.'

'Only three at Derby, Hobhouse?' The occasion was very vivid. Sidmouth was ill at the time – a congestion of the liver – and derived more benefit from the Derby trials than from anything the doctors gave him. His cure was sealed by the letters, many from people he had never heard of, expressing gratitude for the number of convictions. He turned from the window: 'During our time in office we have vindicated the supremacy of the law, have we not? – and satisfied the public that compassion for the few is an injustice to the many.'

Hobhouse at the desk said, 'There remains Manchester.'

Reverting to the window pane, speaking to the cold metropolis, Sidmouth said, 'There remains Manchester . . . ' He was in no doubt that the show of power on St Peter's Fields deserved the country's thanks. Manchester was saved and peace restored at the cost of some criminals consigned to prison, the loss of one day's work and only fifteen lives. He had received a message from the king applauding his forbearance.

Hobhouse untwisted his legs: 'We're trying to hasten the trial of the prisoners taken at Manchester – we shall have them in court within a month.'

'Within a month . . . ' From the minister's tone he would prefer it sooner. 'A capital charge, Hobhouse?'

'Unlawful meeting – they were given warning, I see no difficulty.'

'Unlawful meeting for what purpose?'

'Creating discontent, I fancy – inciting the king's subjects. The trial carries no risk for us.'

'That will be three years' imprisonment at best. I'm not immodest, Hobhouse, but we know the English radical intimately and he would cause worse damage if we didn't sometimes hang him. You know my thinking . . . ' The minister wasn't a pitiless man. His unbending purpose, his tenacity to what he considered right, were tempered by the utmost gentleness to individuals. He was often heard to quote the king – 'Give me the man who judges one human being with severity and every other with indulgence' – and add that indulgence in his case extended to human imperfections. This morning he tried a new quotation on Hobhouse: 'It is an important part of wisdom to know what to overlook,' and returned from the window to his desk.

Hobhouse voiced his minister's thoughts: 'A man gets some brutes together, finds them in pubs or in the streets and scatters a few ideas over their heads, works on their own situation, drags in some event, the mood of the moment, a political topic – it isn't hard for someone who has read a book or two like Thistlewood . . . '

Sidmouth sat down, smitten by that name, unable to remain standing. 'Thistlewood . . . ' Fastidiously he picked it like a fishbone off his tongue and blinked at the memory of an episode that still hurt, a threat not to his person but his courage. It was two years since Thistlewood sent him a challenge to fight with sword or pistol. The cabinet urged him to have Thistlewood prosecuted, but it meant swearing on oath that he had been put in bodily fear, which was perjury. He yielded only when the king persuaded him that it was a form of words and carried no hint of cowardice. But at every report on Thistlewood since leaving prison Sidmouth was taunted by that oath and by a man he had never seen, described as tall and strong and brave, who hovered with a chuckle in the shadows of his consciousness. He said, 'I wonder what he has in mind – the West End job, you say . . . '

'Kick up a row, is what George told me.'

'Ah, George told you . . . ' Hobhouse had promised results from George. But with the secretary's unblinking eyes, those coils and convolutions of the limbs and languid monotones that plumbed the depths of unenthusiasm, it was a marvel that his schemes worked. Sometimes they were deadly.

Hobhouse said, 'But Thistlewood has been frustrated too often, they must do it quickly.'

'A year in prison wasn't enough, or too long if he spent it cultivating grievances.'

'The timing is important – they're watching for their chance. When they see it, when London is off its guard, they must seize it.'

'Seize London, Hobhouse?'

'He claims they can do it in a night.'

Sidmouth clasped his hands and closed his eyes. It was a position he took in church, believing that righteousness suffused his face; certainly there was puzzlement and pain. In time he said, 'It came to me at the privy council yesterday, it was very moving – you would have felt the same, Hobhouse. The king has found a new dignity. The way he spoke to me afterwards, with praise for our arrangements . . . '

'The Manchester trial?'

'That was the moment when I was struck. A sense of history, perhaps. Some of us mercifully are aware. We must preserve, Hobhouse – preserve and take precautions.'

'The elections next month?' The secretary knew his minister's mind.

Sidmouth opened his eyes. They rose slowly to the king's portrait, his voice rising with them: 'We have been in office for thirty years and the king expects us to continue – I have seen it in his smile.' In the painting the royal lips were about to break. 'We mustn't fail, Hobhouse, but we haven't long. You say the timing is important for our friends. Thistlewood and I shall work together – he should be pleased to let me hurry things along.' He slapped the desk and assumed a look of triumph.

There was another question to bring up this morning. Cautiously Hobhouse began, 'George . . . '

'Ah, George – I'm glad you mentioned George.' But gladness didn't show on Sidmouth's face. He walked to the fireplace and

34

stood on the hearthrug: 'I needn't remind you of my feelings . . . '. Then did so, warmed by the fire behind him. 'Secrecy is the element in which our friends exist, therefore we must defeat them through an accomplice – justice requires it.' He paused while Hobhouse began collecting his papers. 'Employing men to foment rebellion would be unforgivable, but when the country is in danger our duty is to adopt every means of getting information.' He almost smiled. 'This has always been the way in England – the law offers impunity and reward to a criminal who contributes to the conviction of his fellows. But such a man is never employed by us in the first place, he seeks us out. The matter lies on his conscience, not ours.' Sidmouth saw Hobhouse's sinuous impatience. 'We have been criticised for it in the past . . . ' He would stop soon, and keep the rest for his journal. 'But if a revolution broke out, who would condemn us more loudly than those who condemned us before?' The question drifted across the room, fading into dust.

Hobhouse didn't answer, he had got what he wanted; picked up his file and went out. Each was familiar with the other's ways.

Sidmouth gave him two minutes, then returned to his desk, took out his journal and pondered his thoughts. One day he would be called to defend himself in the cabinet, perhaps in parliament, and must rehearse his argument: '*The whole tenor of his career – manly, frank, honourable . . .* ' He stopped and tried again. Even Burke had had trouble with his delivery. '*It was fortunate that this unpalatable task fell upon a man so calm, just, wise, fearless, so entirely raised above the influence of unworthy motives. Nothing could be more abhorrent to his nature than to communicate, even indirectly, with someone who was associating with conspirators for the purpose of betraying them. But the security of millions depended on his vigilance.*' He had found a rhythm, he was getting going. '*Devotion to his country alone could hold him to such a task, and he submitted from an overpowering sense of public duty. The perfect candour of his character, innocent of guile or double dealing . . .* '

The chiming Doric clock broke in and Sidmouth's temper flared. But when the last stroke of twelve dwindled in the corners of the room, chasing the echo of his voice, he recovered. The words weren't lost, they would survive in his biography. He sat down and began to write.

Out of nowhere a sudden curiosity touched him: he wanted to see this George. What could such a man be like? But he put it from his mind. Soon it would be lunch.

*

Little Ings hated London, hated it, hated it. From the first of May when he came with his family the place had sickened him. It was a trap you fell into and couldn't get out of. Too big, to start with. No end to it. You couldn't walk into the country and look at the animals, as he did in Portsmouth since he was a boy. Walk up the road and you were in the fields, watching the cows and pigs and country girls. Or you went to the marshes where the sheep were and waited for the tide to come up the creek, wide and quiet and good, or to the harbour to see the ships. Once he wanted to be a sailor in a blue jacket and those trousers, but it didn't last. Too hard in the ships. He heard stories from boys who came back from sea. They had a secret, something you didn't know and they weren't going to tell. Laughed between themselves, somehow unnatural, and went back to sea without saying what it was.

Or you could wait on the jetty for convicts to be marched down the steps and ferried out to the hulks, for transportation. Those steps were the last piece of England they trod on, yet they never lingered. Next soil it would be Australia. The guards didn't drive them down like bullocks, they went meekly into the boat. Even waved to you, rattling their chains. Ings loved England, the bit he knew, and would have struggled. Being packed off for life was terrible to see. He'd rather walk the other way, to the fields. So he became a butcher, to be with animals. Even if it was to kill and cut them up, it was a link. The best job was being sent into the country to bring a bullock back. They gave you dinner in the kitchen with the farm men and let you wander round.

Ings met his wife on a farm. Married a country girl, one he loved, which was more than some could say. It wasn't his fault he never got his own butcher's shop in Portsmouth, which was why he brought the family to London with the money saved. He shouldn't have done it, shouldn't have listened to what people said. It was only for his wife and children, three girls and the boy. One mercy, now they'd gone back his son wouldn't grow up a Londoner. Worse than death, so dirty and noisy, like

Holborn here. Traffic, and people rushing like madmen or doing nothing. You couldn't walk straight for the bumping, pushing, swearing. He'd be glad to see the last of Holborn, the last of this winter afternoon. Glad to get this parcel safe into Fox Court. London did that to you – turned you into a thief. Unthinkable nine months ago. He was an honest man when he came. Nine months it took – the same as a baby. Here was the baby, under his arm. Done up in newspaper, stolen.

He turned into Fox Court. It felt as if he had lived in this hole for ever, not just a week. He was grateful to Brunt for having got the room and paid, but never thought he'd hate a place so much. In Portsmouth nobody would put up with it. In London you'd never get anywhere to live even if you had the money, if you were from the country. You had to know someone. The same in Portsmouth, but you always did know someone, though you were a butcher. In this little backyard you'd never believe you were in the capital of England. Fox Court, they called it, but no fox would come near. They didn't know what one looked like, unless it was Fox the politician. The government was somewhere in this town. Those lords who took away your money, work, food, family. It was a joke – these people the rulers! Couldn't see beyond their crooked noses. Ings loved England, but this wasn't England, this bloody hole.

Up the stairs, the parcel under his arm, hoping not to meet the landlady or Brunt's wife or daughter. Bloody stairs, bloody house, bloody London. But Ings couldn't stay unhappy, he could see the other side. Bloody Brunt, bloody room. The way they treated it! True, Brunt had paid the rent, but they used it as their own, always in it, leaving their things all over. Bloody life, bloody thief. But it was a good cause, the only hope. He was pleased to be useful, working for Mr Thistlewood. There were things a butcher could do. He squeezed the parcel. Bloody stairs.

Entering the room his face was flushed from the cold: 'Here you are – what you asked for.' He opened the parcel to show them. 'Took it from Smithfield, from a butcher when he wasn't looking. I don't like doing it to a butcher but he didn't give me a job last summer, that's why I picked him.' He held out the open paper. A pile of white crystal powder lay on it. 'Saltpetre for meat – to preserve it. On a hot day when you can't get ice. My meat wouldn't have gone bad like it did if I'd been a thief. What d'you want it for, this weather?'

None of them answered. Mrs Brunt's apron was hitched above the window, the dim afternoon struggled through the glass. Thistlewood and Edwards sat by the fire, leaning towards the warmth, Thistlewood on the chair, Edwards on a box. A soldering iron was pushed into the coals under a saucepan of black liquid. Edwards poked the iron, lifted the saucepan to see how it was doing. Thistlewood took snuff. A sword had been left on Ings' bed. Near the window, saving any daylight, the three shoemakers sat on the bench – Brunt, Tidd, Adams – with the black man, Davidson, squatting in front. Tools lay around – nails, bits of iron, sheets of tin, pieces of rope, lampwick, tarred string, a jar of flux. And newspaper spread with two heaps of powder, one black, one yellow.

Ings put his saltpetre on the floor and sat by Davidson: 'I said, what's it for?'

'You'll see,' Brunt told him, with a spoon in his hands. He was uglier than before, more gross with the work.

Adams was cutting tin with shears, his half-dead face twisting to the job; bending the metal to make a can, cutting discs for the top and bottom: 'It goes through as good as leather.'

'We'll try stitching it,' Tidd said. He had lost his shyness in the general activity. 'I don't know what you lot would do without shoemakers.'

'You'll always need a butcher,' Ings said.

Edwards pulled the soldering iron from the fire, red hot, and brought it over. Tidd took it and began soldering the tin. Edwards stopped at the window: 'We should cover it, they can see in.'

Adams said, 'Wait till we light the lamp.'

'We don't want a lamp with this stuff around.' Brunt pointed with his spoon to the coloured powders on the floor. 'Or put your fingers in your ears and wait for the bang.'

Thistlewood and Edwards talked together by the fire, Ings and Davidson watched the shoemakers. Adams cut a narrow tube of tin, Tidd soldered it to the can, Brunt spooned black powder into the can.

'Gunpowder?' Davidson asked.

'Three ounces of the best.' On a piece of newspaper Brunt mixed a spoon of Ings' white crystals with yellow powder, folded the paper for a funnel, poured the mixture into the tube.

'Like filling sausages,' Ings said.

'What's the yellow?' Davidson touched it with a black finger.

Brunt said, 'Brimstone. Mix it with saltpetre for the fuse.' He pushed a piece of lampwick into the tube and held it for Tidd: 'The dodgy part – mustn't have the iron too hot.'

'Say your prayers, Davidson.' Tidd soldered a flap of tin over the top of the can and tube, leaving the end of the wick out. 'Doesn't need to be exact – any gaps we'll seal later.'

'Where did you learn?' Ings asked.

'You thought shoemaking was making shoes.'

'In the army?'

'You want a job, you two?' Brunt gave Ings and Davidson a length of old rope. 'Pull it apart, the strands and the yarn.' He showed them, tearing the hemp into shreds. 'Picking oakum like in prison – good practice for you.'

Tidd laughed recklessly: 'You'll be lucky – if you get rope in Newgate it won't be to pick.' He had recovered. Last week the vision of a scaffold sent a blush of terror into his bald head.

Brunt asked, 'How's the sauce?'

Edwards tilted the saucepan over the fire: 'You want a taste?'

'Fetch it over.' Brunt dipped his spoon into the black liquid, hot and thin. 'It'll do.'

Davidson said, 'Pitch,' with satisfaction. It was his colour.

'And a touch of resin, according to the cook.' With a blacksmith's tongs Brunt picked up the full can and passed it to Adams. Working with Tidd he covered it with a layer of shredded oakum, then smeared it with pitch, layer on layer, the crust hardening as it cooled till the tin was hidden and only the end of the wick stuck out: 'A Duke's dumpling, we call it – you know which Duke.'

'Light the fuse,' Ings said, 'and push it up his arse.'

'Now put the plums in.' Brunt took a handful of nails from the box and pressed them into the outside layer of pitch with his stubby fingers. More oakum, more pitch, more nails. 'Different sizes for different effects – they'll go like bullets.' When it was cool he took it from Adams' tongs and bound the whole thing with a casing of tarred string: 'How's that?' and held it up by the wick – a lethal coconut on a stalk, with a husk an inch thick loaded with shrapnel.

'How long does the fuse burn?' Ings was thinking of the

39

Duke. 'Time to get his trousers off?'

'A foot a minute.' Brunt measured the wick and cut it with the shears to leave two inches: ten seconds.

'How big's the bang?'

Adams said, 'You got a match?' and winked with his single eye.

Brunt wrapped the grenade in paper: 'Next one won't take so long,' and put it in the cupboard behind the pikes. 'Another day we'll make fireballs – oakum and pitch rolled up with brimstone like a doughnut. Throw one of those through a window and you've got a house on fire. Under the furniture or where they keep the wood or into a stable – you can do a lot of harm. A fireball will burn for three minutes if you make it right, and it takes more than that to get the fire engine.' He looked through the window at the dwindling afternoon: 'Time for one more before dark.'

Edwards put the saucepan back on the fire. Thistlewood drew his chair closer, turned up his collar, watched the young artist.

'Bite the hand that doesn't feed you,' Edwards said.

'No revolution was won without violence.'

'It can only come from underneath and we'll get no help. Those old professionals will sell us out, the same as the rich ones. Use us to serve themselves.'

Thistlewood took snuff: 'The ordinary ways are useless, they got us nowhere.' He sounded disappointed or only tired.

'We must improvise, experiment . . . ' A gleam rose in Edwards' eyes, brighter than the fire.

'That's the best thing in a revolution – to invent.'

'Something fantastic, a leap of the imagination . . . '

'It's what you see ahead – the possibilities.'

*

Mrs Brunt stood in the doorway. The men were unaware of her at first, they simultaneously caught her watching them: too late to hide the grenade they were making, snatch the sword off Ings' bed, shut the cupboard door on the bundle of pikes. They hadn't lit the lamp and by the feeble winter light there was a hope that she hadn't seen what they were doing or hadn't understood. Her face said nothing. The impassive, weary eyes of a woman for whom no fresh view of a battered life was too unlikely: not yet middle-aged but beyond the ability to be shocked.

'I told you to knock,' Brunt shouted, his fright growing quickly into anger. 'Not to come in here – there's nothing for you.' He turned to the others to show his indignation: he wasn't responsible for his wife: 'I told her . . .'

Davidson whistled softly, Ings nudged him to stop. Thistlewood took a pinch of snuff, Edwards stared into the fire, Tidd began picking things off the floor. Nobody knew how to deal with this. Adams was the most agitated. The blacksmith's tongs rattled in his hands, his crooked face blanched, his mouth hung sideways. The sunken left eye was lodged on something invisible at his feet, his right eye transfixed the figure of Mrs Brunt in horror.

'I wondered what you were up to, that's all,' she said. 'You spend all day and never tell me. I only wanted to see.' She spoke calmly, not to her husband alone, and stood looking at them without coming into the room. 'It's not shoemaking.' She simply observed a fact: the piles of powder, tin and nails and pitch and string, the unfamiliar smell – it wasn't shoemaking.

The menace could be returned. Brunt went towards her like an animal, his fist clenched on the unfinished grenade. She looked him in the face, defiant and spent. He stopped a few inches short, his big jaw jutting into hers: 'Get out!' through his teeth.

Her focus only shifted, she looked through him into the room: 'I wanted to see.'

He could stop her entering but couldn't stop her looking. It drove him to savagery. He lifted the fist with the grenade, swung it into her chest, forcing her back on to the dark landing, and in the same swing punched the door shut. A thud was heard outside, but the sigh that followed might have come from one of the men. Helpless, outraged, Brunt turned on them: 'I told her . . .'

Nobody moved or spoke, the only sound was the shiver of the tongs in Adams' hand. Brunt's scowl challenged them to accuse him. Through the door they heard the woman pick herself up and move into the front room where she lived. Roughly Brunt took the tongs and gave them to Tidd; then finished the grenade alone, daubing it with pitch and nails and binding it with string while the others watched. When it was done he lit a taper from the fire and put it to the lamp. Life, frozen by Mrs Brunt's appearance, thawed with the glow of light.

Little Ings sat down cheerfully on his bed, the master of his premises: 'My wife's in Portsmouth, she won't blow in like that.'

Brunt said, 'Holy fucking Christ, mine won't again, not after that,' and tossed his chin towards the door.

'We must be careful,' Thistlewood warned. 'People will talk and then it's finished.'

'She won't talk – I'll settle that,' Brunt growled, his face still brutalised.

Ings said, 'They're already talking. The landlady asked me what's going on, with men always in and out and carrying things. Other people were wondering too. There were two gentlemen that came about a room to let, but it wasn't their real reason, she saw they weren't the sort to want a room. She asked me, was it a club? was it radicals? was it anarchists? Trying to get it out of me and I wasn't saying. I was suspicious she wanted it for passing to the two who called.'

'You should have told us before,' Edwards said. 'If you hear anything you must tell Mr Thistlewood.' The young artist could be stern and responsible.

Tidd said, 'Like Mr Thistlewood says, you can't keep a thing quiet. So we must get on with it and not waste time. Every day we put it off is a risk, I say.' Tidd surprised himself with his audacity.

In his slanting voice Adams said, 'Those gentlemen who came – I saw them downstairs and told myself, those are from Bow Street, not a jot of doubt.' Adams had come out of prison, he knew a policeman when he saw one. 'You get to know them, there's a look in them that's different – you can't say what.'

Ings said, 'Time to get on with it.'

'Time to move from here,' Thistlewood said. Fox Court was dangerous, and too far from the West End. They must get a place closer to the job where men and weapons could be assembled without being observed: somewhere without a landlady on the stairs or a wife standing in the door. It could all be wrecked by carelessness.

Edwards was thinking the same: 'I heard of somewhere, a stable in a mews. Cato Street, by the Horse and Groom.'

'I know the Horse and Groom,' Adams said, 'between

Oxford Street and Edgware Road – the landlord was a friend.' He couldn't control the shake that crept into his voice.

'There's a loft above, where we could go,' Edwards told them. 'I was offered it for a studio and I'd take it, it's quiet and plenty of room.'

Thistlewood was thankful for Edwards. He had most of the ideas, most of the answers. The older man watched the young rebel partly with pleasure, partly nostalgia. There was a style about him which the rest, for all their zeal and ingenuity, couldn't match: a touch of class. He was respectable, almost urbane. It would be useful later in a people's government. None of the other men could have produced a stable in the West End. Thistlewood decided: 'We'll go and see it.' He stood up and his green eyes reflected the soft flame of the lamp; illuminated the start of a new hope.

*

. . . I see the crowds in the palace gardens and the Champs Elysées. Refreshment stalls, pantomimes and puppets, music and singing and dancing. There was a feeling of suspension, life was interrupted, reality was put aside. Clothilde asked if it could happen in London, and I said only if habeas corpus and the law courts were abolished. Paris was on holiday, except the prisoners in the Abbaye – nobles, priests, the remnants of the Swiss guards, hundreds of men and women who had been arrested though there was nothing against them, but nothing in their favour except their innocence. Could the people in the streets be as happy as they looked? Clothilde said they were as happy as the gods, and took my hand to come and look at a performing monkey. If you called it an aristocrat the monkey flew at your throat and pulled your hair, but if you called it a patriot it smiled and kissed you.

Walking near the Abbaye once I saw the pack of killers waiting for another victim. They had three dripping wagon-loads of corpses to show what sport it was, and drank from jugs of wine, sharpened their blades, howled like dogs when the door opened. The creature standing there in horror and the axe crashing into its skull and the swords driven into its stomach – it was something I was told about or perhaps dreamed. The creature was a white-haired proud old man, and a drooling priest, and a fair girl younger than myself whose screams

43

followed me for years, and a Swiss soldier who clicked his heels smartly in the doorway before leading his friends unarmed into the pack.

. . . I see the head of a young woman on a pike, with hooting patriots dragging what was left of her body. The long brown hair, open mouth, furious eyes – I had seen them before, if only I could remember where. Later, in the Hôtel de Moscovie when Clothilde was telling me the day's news, it came to me – the face of the beautiful lady-in-waiting, the fairy tale princess who had sat in the little panelled box with the royal family and flushed with anger when they were cursed for the miseries of France. My remorse drained away, with Clothilde's help.

. . . I see the inevitability of events. At the time, a stranger just arrived in Paris, I couldn't know the truth about the treason the king was charged with, but I saw the need for charging him. The people had been told of the great example which France must show, they were fed with the idea of their king being tried for his life, they couldn't be let down. Accounts of King Charles I's trial were hastily put on sale and any Englishman was treated as an expert. An Englishman in Paris – yet England and France were at war. I saw the king being taken back to prison after his trial, and felt the shock of this mild doomed man at the window of a coach, resigned to some necessity yet unaware of guilt, keeping his composure in spite of soldiers and cannons and the shouting people everywhere. But I didn't go that January morning to the guillotine. Clothilde told me how he took off his coat, unbuttoned his shirt, went to the edge of the scaffold and held up his hand for silence. The crowd, struck at last by what they were doing and more agitated than the king, obeyed. He spoke only a few words before an officer ordered the drums to drown his voice, he was grabbed by six butchers and tied down to the plank. The priest kneeling at the king's head, praying with him, had his own face splashed with blood. Describing it with a little fart between her lips Clothilde said it was like any other Paris day.

. . . I see a sombre prison somewhere else, with flanking towers, shot holes, iron spikes jutting above the gates, chains hanging on the walls. And my cell, as if cut from solid rock. I have known other cells – this was three yards long, two yards wide, with a half moon grating for a window. From a ledge I could touch the bars. I can remember the smell.

. . . I see Robespierre, high priest of the Jacobins, the strict man with a creed among less rigid men buffeted by ideas. He could be excited by the universe, testing his beliefs like an astronomer, or a barren long-winded bore. Someone shouted to him to stop the harangue but he went on for another hour. He boasted of his patriotism and honesty, he challenged his enemies to attack him, knowing that to be in danger was to be loved, and defended himself brilliantly, to the gallery's applause. Popularity was his passion, he would surrender all ambition for it. He spoke of man being born for liberty and happiness but doomed to slavery and misery. He called for a republic with votes for all citizens, demanded a military purge, claimed that the law was the people's sovereign will, cried for universal education, promised a state in which men of all nations were brothers and nobody was excluded who believed in the rights of others.

. . . I see him emotional and outraged in parliament, logical and implacable in the Jacobins Club, anaemic and melancholy in his room in the Rue St Honoré. I gave up hoping for his friendship but still went there to hear him talk, and once he chided me for being an Englishman. My English king with his ministers and lackeys were deceived by the French revolution, too immoral to believe in the people's virtue, too stupid to take one step towards the future. They were lagging behind the century they lived in, for it was heading for liberty and they wanted to drag it back to barbarity and despotism . . . I see Robespierre's eyes fixed on mine, accusing me of England's failure, daring me to denounce tyranny and believe in the infallible people's will. I dared, and always shall.

. . . I see, years later, hundreds of Englishmen from the Lancashire factories streaming into the fields and hills. We mustered in squads and drilled in the sweet country air. Old sergeants and corporals brought from retirement gladly gave the orders – falling in, dressing by the right, turning about, wheeling. Down the English lanes, through the woods in the dusk or before dawn on Sunday, marching in the mist. Our breath in the cold air, boots wet with dew, the scent of flowers and new hay growing out of the night. We saluted the sun climbing over a hill and women came up from the farms with milk cans, bread, apples, bottles of beer. A lucky favoured youth might slink into the morning landscape with a girl. Then the bugle call for more drill. We had no arms – a man would cut a stick from the hedge, another had a swagger cane. Up and down under the old campaigners, standing at ease in the early sunshine, arranging boxing matches on the wet grass, wrestling, jumping, racing. The excitement of a new day with young men, and talk of economics, foreign policy, atheism, deism. Cigarettes were passed round, books and pamphlets pulled out with the Sunday papers.

. . . I see the march setting out from Manchester to London. Three hundred started, out of ten thousand at the meeting, when the Riot Act was read and we were broken up by soldiers. A train of ragged, shuffling people with a petition for parliament – I pitied and loved them. Some had decent clothes and bags of food and bottles, and one man had a violin. Mostly they were a shivering patched-up lot, unprepared for the gentle, bitter, sopping rain. Next to me was a young man and his wife, thin and pale with her baby in a blanket. After a few hours she was defeated. The man hugged and squeezed the baby and kissed his wife, who stood abandoned by the road. Marching on to London he spoke of the dark room without coal or food where she would wait for him in fear and hope. But it wouldn't be so bad again – London was more than a promise, it was the future.

A battalion of soldiers had blocked a bridge and some of the marchers gave up – they knew what soldiers did. The rest got over the river, with one man shot and several wounded, and that night a hundred and eighty marched into Macclesfield, a tenth of the way to London. Some found lodgings, some went to prison, others slept in the market place or crept home without a word. Next day only twenty marched and on the second night we were nine. So the march was over and England saved.

*

Nobody could remember such a winter as this of 1820. At midday on a Sunday in February, though the snow had gone from the roofs and gutters, the sky was heavy with more. The long passage had never been so bleak and most people had battened down their lives. In a month, six weeks, two months it would be behind them.

Expectancy reached the stable in Cato Street, stirring behind the blacked-out windows of the loft, but the twenty men up there were irritable with inactivity. Morose and sullen himself,

Thistlewood saw the moodiness of the others: the hardest winter of their lives – he would show that it needn't come again. He must convince them and hope that they could hold out. They had a safe meeting place, more men had joined, their stock of weapons and ammunition was growing, they only needed a plan.

'Christianity was born in a stable,' Davidson said. He had been a preacher in Jamaica and knew how to please Thistlewood. Through the floor a vestige of stale manure rose from the fusty disused stalls, bringing a sort of promise. The cracks and knot holes in the boards were vital: someone entering from the street could be heard upstairs and challenged. Harrison, a veteran sentry from the army, invented the password – 'Sid', and the reply, 'mouth'. If it failed a grenade would be thrown down. The ladder was the last defence. Anyone coming up through the hatch would appear head first: 'We'll top him like a pineapple,' Davidson said.

Hop sacks and bits of canvas were hung over the windows, cracked panes had been patched with paper, cobwebs left in place. No light came in, nothing went out. The damp air, thick with the odours of twenty men, the sour whiff from below, the fumes of tobacco and candles and the oil stove, couldn't be freshened from outside. Pieces of harness, heaps of straw, rotten boots lay in the dark corners with swords, pistols, grenades, fireballs, flannel powder bags. Pikes were stacked on the rafters. In the middle a trestle table was set up with old chairs and stools.

Today's president of the revolution committee, Tidd, once a shoemaker, sat at the end of the table with a broken pike in his hand and two candles in front. The men took turns as president, it was democratic and good practice, but Tidd was unsure what to do. Thistlewood sat on his right for comfort and advice, Brunt on his left. Beyond Thistlewood were Edwards, Adams, Harrison the soldier, Cooper the sailor. Opposite were Davidson, Ings, Bradburn and three whom Thistlewood hardly knew – Gilchrist, Wilson and Strange. At the far end or standing at the back were others, the most that had ever come. The candles and a lamp lit their faces against the dim walls of the loft.

'The world has been interpreted by philosophers, too many of them,' Thistlewood said. 'They have their ideas, some good,

47

some false, but interpreting the world is finished – the thing now is to change it.' He looked down the table and back to Tidd: 'Are we agreed, Mr President, that we must make a plan?'

Uncertainly Tidd echoed, 'A plan . . . '

'I'm sick of waiting for this job, we must attack, we've got to kill them,' little Ings said. 'I borrowed ten shillings to send to Portsmouth, I've got nothing now.'

Edwards, who had lent the money, told him, 'All speeches must be addressed to the president.' He could show how a committee worked.

Thistlewood went on: 'We can't get them in parliament or Downing Street and they've stopped their cabinet dinners.'

Ings said, 'Invite them to dinner here,' holding two straws in his hands like a knife and fork. 'Sidmouth on my right, Castlereagh on my left, the Duke . . . ' and caught a scowl from Brunt that silenced him.

'We can't get them together,' Thistlewood decided, 'so it must be one by one in their homes. We won't get as many that way – three at the most.'

'Three?' The president questioned the faces like an auctioneer calling for a higher bid. He looked unhappy and dropped his broken pike on the floor. Thistlewood put on a wistful smile while the men talked, clenching their teeth and fists.

'Three's not enough, we must chop the lot.'

'Depends on how many we can muster.'

'It'll take fifty men.'

'A hundred, more like.'

'The Irish off the building sites who can't get work – they'll join if it's against the government.'

'There's a lot that lives in Gee's Court near Oxford Circus.'

'There's a pub in Wigmore Street where they go, the Pomfret Castle.'

'Never trust the Irish, they'll do nothing till they see the English start it, they've been deceived too often.'

'Settle which ministers are to be chopped and who's to do it.'

'We need the men or else . . . '

'I'll bring twenty, no trouble.'

'Bring all we can and give them food.'

'Food!'

'Bread and cheese and beer – I'll see to that.'

'I tell you, man, they'll ask what they're wanted for and what's the plan and when it's to be done.'

'They'll be suspicious, they'll betray it.'

'I have a proposal, Mr President . . .'

Thistlewood pointed to Brunt, jogging Tidd who picked up his broken pike and banged the table.

Brunt stood up: 'I propose we form platoons like in the army for doing them in their homes, and one man's given the job and if he fails it's the next man.'

'A man can try his best and fail,' Adams said, hoping with his single eye to prop his tottering courage.

'Anyone who fails,' Brunt said, 'holy fucking Christ, he'll be killed himself,' and sat down, wiping the back of his fist across his lips.

'Give them three days,' Thistlewood announced. 'Go to work on Wednesday night if we don't see a better chance.'

'The Revolution of February the Twenty-third.'

'Chop the lot at home and burn their houses.'

'Sidmouth lives in a fancy place he got given by the king.'

'For the men he hanged at York.'

'The Archbishop of York lives in Grosvenor Square.'

'The Bishop of London's as bad as any.'

'Lord Castlereagh's in St James's Square.'

'They're all in church today, praying for themselves.'

'They need to.'

Thistlewood said, 'Once we've done the ministers and started fires and the news gets round, it'll become a general thing.'

'Soon as something's being done the people will be with us.'

'Soldiers too.'

'There's two cannons at the post in Gray's Inn, six at the Artillery Ground . . .'

'We'll have London by the morning.'

'We've got powder for cartridges but no cannonballs.'

'Iron railings – knock the tops off, man.'

'Cooper's in charge of the cannon party – put them round parliament, the Mansion House . . .'

'Force it to surrender or open fire.'

'Plunder the Bank of England.'

'But not destroy the books, so we can find out who has property.'

'Harrison's in charge of the fire party – set them off with fireballs and we'll have a lot on fire by breakfast time.'

'Breakfast at Lord Sidmouth's for me, with the old bugger's carcase under the table getting cold and Lady Sidmouth pouring out the tea.'

'She's been dead for years.'

'He'll be with her soon.'

'Fifty men, you say, to do the ministers and take the cannons and start the fires – but where d'you find them?'

'One man can do it alone, he'll get the whole of fucking England behind him.'

They knew which man Brunt meant.

Tidd banged his broken pike more confidently: 'Are we agreed?'

They thumped and stamped and held up fists: 'Agreed, agreed . . . '

Twenty men pumped hands across the table, clapped shoulders, swore oaths of brotherhood and freedom. In the reeking loft Thistlewood's green eyes shone with a luminous revelation when Ings, flushed almost to tears, grabbed his hand and shook it violently. A glow of emotion struggled into his enigmatic face, he hadn't heard men talk of action like this before. In the dark stable he saw the thrill that lit their lives, the power in their hands.

*

There was a feeling of replenishment on Monday morning. The Doric clock had been wound up and would go for seven days.

Lord Sidmouth, who had been to church twice yesterday, also felt wound up, taut with energy and inspiration. The king never worked on Sunday either and it was a pity that other ministers didn't follow the royal example; Lord Castlereagh was the worst. It was another pity that Castlereagh's habits betrayed the most ignoble influences of these times: twenty-five years of marriage and no children, which couldn't be due only to the fatness of Lady Castlereagh. There wasn't much to be said for Castlereagh's private life, except that it was a pity . . .

Sidmouth checked his thoughts. This feeling of replenishment: it reached through Hobhouse to the secretaries and clerks down to the lowest messenger. The mainspring was tight again, the ministry would run for another week, this week into next, February into March, spring into summer; he allowed the staff a short summer holiday because they worked better after it, though for himself he took only the church festivals and three days in August to spend with his grandchildren by the sea . . .

Again he checked himself; took the journal from its drawer, stood up and spoke: '*The difficulty was to decide how far the evil should be allowed to grow. He mustn't interfere too soon, but in time to prevent catastrophe.*' He had been rehearsing over the weekend and some of the phrases had come to him at evensong. '*Unless the threat was far enough advanced to indicate great danger to the country the public might not be convinced.*' He looked at the clock: Hobhouse would be waiting to be called in. '*When the threat was passed, nothing was more common than for the public to look back on it with contempt. In any rebellion that failed, the danger was forgotten and its existence doubted. So it was imperative to allow this plot to reach a point at which its gravity could be most widely felt.*' He sat down, copied it into his journal, put it back in the drawer and picked up the silver bell: 'Well, Hobhouse.' It was the daily tuning-up for their duet. 'Our friends – what news today?'

Tortuously the secretary arranged his limbs and documents; took a paper from a file, put it back, took another and a third and at last was ready: 'I have some of their names.'

'Their names . . .'

'One of them is Brunt.'

'Brunt . . . ' The minister savoured it like a peppercorn, small but explosive.

'A shoemaker.'

'Ah . . . ' Shoemakers were seldom dangerous.

'And his friend Ings.'

'What names these people choose! Can you conceive of a man called Ings? Tell me, what are . . . ?' Sidmouth's high voice dropped a semitone but his joke withered to a tiny smile: 'What is Ings?'

'A butcher out of work, and there's another shoemaker – Tidd.'

'Heavens, these cobblers! And a butcher! I tremble for my life. And yours, Hobhouse. And our country.' Sidmouth got to his feet and went to the window. 'What mercy can we expect? Shall we hurl ourselves at their feet? Shall we flee? But where? – oh God, to France!' Sidmouth hadn't been there and never

51

wished to, but he had a clear view of it. France was the source of that malignant Jacobin spirit which had brought disgrace to England. Like any foreign mischief, like a disease, it worked its way into the weak spots of the English character. In the war, when soldiers and sailors were raising England to pinnacles of glory, it had detracted from their victories and exaggerated the enemy's virtues. Since then it had blamed every calamity on the government and taught its deluded followers that their grievances could be cured by violence. But through vigilance – keeping watch on anyone coming across the Channel, banning meetings of more than fifty people, confiscating arms and flags, controlling newspapers, seizing libellous publications, suppressing blasphemy and sedition, suspending habeas corpus – the government had rescued England from the fate of France.

Hobhouse read out more names: 'Adams, Cooper, Harrison . . . '

'Ah, some polysyllables,' the minister said, watching the people in Whitehall and turning his mind to greater things. He had spoken to the king at the time when thousands were threatening to march from Manchester to London with some vague petition, and his majesty was reminded of that other march from Marseilles to Paris. Sidmouth took the hint: the army was called in.

'Wilson, Strange, Gilchrist . . . '

If only Burke's wisdom had been heeded – 'let us keep French principles from our heads and French daggers from our hearts' – the country would have been spared half the wickedness that plagued it. The French had a lot to answer for and other foreigners were no better: for them a knife or revolver were as normal as a walking-stick or tobacco pouch to an Englishman. Unfortunately the English gave asylum to a crowd of undesirables – Latins, Slavs, orientals, blacks – who were living here on charity and their wits . . . But Sidmouth must attend to the secretary: 'You got these names from . . . ?'

'From George – he goes to their meetings.'

'Ah, George . . . ' It was gratifying to hear of Hobhouse's success.

'Bradburn, Davidson . . . '

'Never mind their names, Hobhouse – what are they, these people? Not all cobblers?'

The secretary ran a finger down the list: 'Tailor, carpenter, shop assistant, chair maker, sailor . . . '

'Ah, that kind of thing – I begin to understand.'

'Davidson is a black man.' Hobhouse knew what such a fact could do.

'A black man . . . ' Sidmouth repeated it with abomination: it was disgusting, profane, against his nature and religion, something he wouldn't touch if it wasn't his duty. Gravely he returned to the desk: 'You know my feelings, Hobhouse – we must be careful this time. We have never let ourselves be confused by crude appeals for humanity.' He sat down and closed his eyes: it was easier to see a black man with them shut. When one was mentioned he liked a short silence, just as at the name of God or Jesus or the king or Lady Sidmouth he paused for a private blessing. With a black man it was for a curse.

Hobhouse knew what was going on behind the eyelids, also what was in the desk. One day this minister, at the mercy of party and king and electorate, would depart and another come, but a secretary was unaffected by fickle human sentiments and must watch the ministry's lasting interests. Hobhouse did it well. He had read the journals secretly, noting the important passages, and could see which one Sidmouth was reciting to himself.

With his eyes shut Sidmouth was busy with a point that might trouble his biographer if he was to give the right impression: *'Early in his life he decided that there was no conflict between politics and the Christian faith. Perhaps his popularity was damaged by his stand against the abolition of the slave trade, but his conscience never required him to regret it. Certainly he wanted to see decent regulations for the slave ships and decent punishments for any captain guilty of wanton brutality, but to prohibit the trade was to drive it out of reach of parliament and worsen the pathetic situation of the blacks. The bill was passed due to the agitation of a few Quakers and evangelists and other dissenters from the established church, but mercifully it was only the slave trade, not slavery, that was abolished. He trusted that his children and grandchildren wouldn't live to see Englishmen in the colonies forced to surrender the source of their prosperity by troublemakers at home with no experience of the realities and no motive higher than plain envy. It would be the ruin of the empire.'*

Hobhouse judged the moment; then, as quickly as he could for a man incapable of speed, began fussing with his papers.

But Sidmouth hadn't finished: *'He was the last men to deny that there was a force of change at work, which he would no more denounce than any other scheme of Providence, but he believed that slaves should be allowed to buy their freedom in degrees with the money they earned by their own labour. Because of the need for many black men to do the work of one white man and the dangers of overpaying them it would be generations before they could save the price of their ransom, and the time should be devoted to improving their temporal condition and preparing them for freedom. More churches should be built in the colonies as the first step towards civilisation. The blacks should be instructed in Christian morality and their families properly united by the ties of matrimony. Eventually, in some unimaginable future, he foresaw the possibility of the children of slaves being free and educated at public expense like children in the orphanages of England . . .'*

He opened his eyes: 'What do they talk about? – these tinkers, tailors, black men . . . '

Hobhouse shrugged and tried to guess: 'Politics? Personalities? Revolutionaries have their heroes in their fashion – Thomas Paine, William Cobbett, Rousseau . . . '

'Mere names, I suppose, to many of them. I mean, Rousseau to a butcher . . . '

Hobhouse said, 'They've given themselves till Wednesday.'

'Today is Monday.' Sidmouth listened to Hobhouse's report. His mind, like a secretariat with specialists and archivists and old files for reference, absorbed it and planned a strategy. There might be younger minds in Whitehall, but he was gratified by his own, and admired the workings. Over the years he had tended it and rectified its imperfections till he was in possession of a machine as fine as any in the country which, like the journal in his desk, he would offer for the country's use.

He surveyed the proportions of his office, the august portraits, dignified furniture and tall windows. Which of the conspirators would sit here – one of the cobblers, the butcher, the common sailor? And Hobhouse – would he serve a black man? But if Sidmouth allowed himself a shudder it was far from fear. Fear was weakness, which he had been spared. Pity was his first emotion on hearing how other men in London had spent their Sunday; then outrage. The absurdity of the plot was exceeded by its criminality. He could only take it seriously when he recalled other schemes of Thistlewood's. Now that benighted creature and his friends, in a stable in some obscure street which Sidmouth was thankful never to have heard of, had delusions of upsetting the monarchy on Wednesday night and turning England into a republic . . . A happier thought occurred to him. Last week at the privy council the king had appeared listless, his perception slack, his command of affairs weak. Sidmouth suspected insomnia and suggested a remedy that his late wife had found helpful – a pillow filled with hops. Today he had been handed a note from the palace saying that his majesty was already sleeping better.

Hobhouse finished his report, and waited. It was hard to tell his feelings or even if he had any.

Sidmouth said, 'There is one point . . . ' He looked sharply across the desk, hoping that the point was registered, but the secretary's face gave nothing away. The minister continued: 'It's my one anxiety – if our friends suspect that they are discovered . . . ' He stopped again, ashamed to ask for reassurance.

Hobhouse was more than disappointed, assuming the nearest thing to pain that he could manage, and dropped his voice to a tone of sorrow, a hollow whisper of perplexity and disbelief: 'I think we can rely on George,' and blinked rapidly to show the depth of his injury, then let his eyes settle sweetly on the minister to suggest forgiveness.

'Ah, George . . . ' Often there was a suspicion among criminals that one of them would betray the rest to save himself – a suspicion to be encouraged as it destroyed all confidence between them. The Luddite gangs had taken oaths not to give away an accomplice and to kill anyone who did, but they had been crushed in the end. This lot were made of less fanatical stuff. Sidmouth was tempted to muse on the curious identity of George, the worm in the woodwork, but it was time to move on: 'Hobhouse, you know my feelings . . . '

Hobhouse knew them well. He could follow the minister's mind step by step, complete each unfinished sentence to the word and anticipate the next. He curled his legs round the chair, worked his long fingers in front of him like knitting needles and said, 'Precisely.'

'It's a carbuncle that collects poison from the blood, which must be allowed to grow to the point of eruption before it can be lanced . . . '

'The point of greatest danger.'

But Sidmouth wasn't afraid of Thistlewood, he feared only

God: 'If we operate too soon and lose the poison and let it drain back . . . '

'There are two more days.'

'If we arrest them today and bring them to trial on the evidence we have and fail to convince a jury and let them loose in triumph . . . '

'With better luck next time.'

'We risk the public imagining it to be our invention.'

'Or the work of an agent.'

'If we delay too long and await the attack on the ministers at home . . . ' Sidmouth waited for the secretary to interrupt, but there was silence. 'We expose ourselves to the consequences.' He stood up and walked to the window: 'If we allow them to proceed unmolested to the brink of action and arrest them under circumstances which leave no doubt of guilt . . . ' He looked down into Whitehall, searching for something he knew was there. In the traffic, among the people, was the particle to fertilise an idea already poised to receive it.

'Precisely,' Hobhouse said.

Two men walked past, hunched in their coats. One looked up to the window, caught the minister's eye, spoke to the other who waved. They laughed together and Sidmouth was transfixed by an insult though no word reached him. A woman crossed the street, with her child skipping hand in hand. A policeman on horseback ambled towards Parliament Square. A sweeper pushed a broom along the gutter, doing a good job so long as he was content with what he got and didn't snatch more, because, as the king once said, man could not create abundance where Providence had inflicted scarcity. A sailor appeared on the far side of the street – lame, perhaps wounded, moving his weight to each foot as if not trusting them. A leg buckled and he landed in the gutter; staggered to lean against a water trough, missed it, barged into the sweeper, opened his mouth to speak to a lamp post, but vomited. Sidmouth had a horror of drink, he was revolted by this Monday morning obscenity in Whitehall. He must ring for a messenger to drive the sailor away or bring back the policeman. But he only watched in contempt and fascination. The sweeper propped his broom against his barrow to rub his hand and spit – he was a cripple with one arm and Sidmouth recognised him. On his late wife's birthday he had given the man some coins, among them

56

by mistake a half sovereign. Next day in the street the sweeper opened his tobacco box and gave it back. Sidmouth was offended at such a person's honesty, it was improper. He took the half sovereign, remembering it was no longer Lady Sidmouth's birthday, and never gave the sweeper money again – the man had let him down. But today his disgust was kept for the sailor, kissing the foot of the lamp post. Sidmouth had to call on his sense of perspective, his vision of history as he had witnessed it. He had been prime minister, had been taken into the king's confidence, had carried Burke's coffin and spoken to Nelson, and now sat in the cabinet with the Duke of Wellington . . .

But Hobhouse mustn't be kept all morning. Sidmouth turned from the window: 'We are decided,' and walked back across the room. 'I have always been a peaceful man.' He caught the merest nod from the secretary who was picking up his papers. 'I haven't wilfully given pain to any human being.' He sat down and closed his eyes, to pause like a pilgrim on the threshold of his conscience, then opened them and continued quietly: 'I'm confident that the loyal classes are satisfied with the way in which their trust in me has been honoured.' Aware that Hobhouse knew what was coming he arranged his words in order: 'In times of insurrection it has been our policy to employ the police alone and call in the army for such an emergency as we had at Manchester. When they opened fire it had a magical effect. Only thirty shots were needed to disperse the crowd.'

Hobhouse released a gesture, a tilt of the head as if disturbed by an itching collar, to show that he understood: 'The barracks in Portman Square will be convenient – the Coldstream Guards will be ordered to have a picket at a moment's notice.'

'A moment's notice – it would be a comfort to know that it means exactly that. I needn't add . . .'

'Without exciting the suspicions of Thistlewood.' Subtly Hobhouse showed the difficulty of controlling himself. A movement of the fingers, another convolution of the legs, even a total arrest of visible life, could convey his impatience to deal with the final point and be free to leave.

The message reached Sidmouth: 'It's a dinner party they're waiting for.' He looked into the secretary's face, hoping to read surprise or admiration. 'Will you see to that? – if they're so

57

hungry, let them have a dinner.'

Hobhouse said, 'Invitations will be sent.'

*

A voice shouted 'Sid' from the bottom of the ladder and someone above answered 'mouth'. A man should be standing by the ladder with a sword to see who was coming up, but the drill had slipped.

It was Edwards, in the old brown coat, stepping off the ladder and peering round, a newspaper in his hand. 'Good morning!' Coming from the street into the light of a few candles and one lamp he couldn't see much. With a grunt of welcome Thistlewood made room at the table.

Harrison said, 'Time to change the password,' but there was no enthusiasm. In the smoke of apathy and stench of pessimism the men brooded irritably and quarrelled. The revolution would break out tomorrow night, a day and a half away, yet they hadn't decided on the platoons to attack the cabinet ministers or which ones to pick.

Thistlewood asked, 'What's in the paper?' and Edwards spread it on the table by the lamp. The two began reading out the news: most of the others couldn't read.

'*Lord Dewhurst, son of the Earl of Coventry, arrived yesterday at the Pulteney Hotel, Piccadilly from his father's seat in Worcestershire, also Miss Talkington from Yorkshire . . .*'

'It's where I stay when I'm in town,' little Ings said. 'Only the very best for the very best.'

Brunt said, 'Just a fancy fucking brothel.'

'*The Marquis and Marchioness of Huntley have returned from a visit to the Marquis and Marchioness of Tavistock . . . Lord and Lady Gordon are the only residents of importance at the palace . . .*'

'Tell that to the king.'

'*Gentleman missing from home since Sunday, aged twenty-seven, five feet nine, in dejected spirits, wearing a black suit, without whiskers, inclined to a florid complexion, a little deaf and frequently coughs . . . A duel took place near the third milestone on the Kilburn road between Captain A. and Mr B., the latter having imputed to the Captain ungentlemanly conduct towards his sister . . . On Saturday evening two men entered the shop of Mr William Drew, one of them went into the parlour where Mrs Drew was sitting and struck her violently on the head and threatened that if she raised the alarm he would knock her brains out,*' *while the other stole an insurance policy for a thousand pounds, a gold sovereign and thirty-five pounds in bank notes . . .* '

'Where's the sports page?'

'*Hounds drew a large fox in Footland Wood, Sussex, which made for Lord Ashburnham's strongholds, but being closely pressed he was obliged to try his strength over the uncovered field and was killed after a gallant chase of three hours and five minutes, when dead this remarkable animal weighed sixteen and a half pounds . . . The fight between Belasco the Jew and Samson the Birmingham youth will take place on the usual swampy piece of ground near the twentieth milestone on the Epping road, betting six to four on the Jew . . .* '

'Wait till you see the papers on Thursday – they'll have something to write about.'

'*Any respectable youth, from fourteen to sixteen years of age, may have a genteel, permanent and confidential situation with a gentleman, the hours of attendance are short, a deposit of a hundred pounds will be asked . . .* '

'That's for Lord Castlereagh.'

'*To be sold by auction at Mr Sotheby's house, the library of a gentleman, together with mahogany bookcases . . . Calico shirts from thirty-eight shillings a dozen, muslin cravats, jean jackets and trousers . . . Genuine Westphalia hams of the finest flavour, twenty pence per pound, pickled reindeer tongues, Russian caviare, Brunswick sausages, Bengal mangoes, Stilton cheeses from the best dairies, Lowestoft red herrings . . .* '

'Holy fucking Christ, is it necessary?'

'*The king received visits from the Dukes of York and Sussex, the Duchess of Gloucester, Prince Leopold and the Marchioness of Cholmon-deley . . . The Earl of Harrowby, lord president of the council, will give a cabinet dinner tomorrow at his house in Grosvenor Square . . .* '

'How about that?'

'What?'

'Read it out.'

'When?'

'There! – a cabinet dinner.'

Thistlewood leant over to read the paragraph above Edwards' finger: 'Tomorrow.'

A surprise assault on the loft couldn't have stirred the men so quickly.

'Wednesday the twenty-third.'

'They've stopped their dinners, it's a hoax.'

'It's in the paper, it says so – *The Times*.'

'Where?'

'Number 44, Grosvenor Square.'

Brunt snatched the paper to read it for himself, then slammed it on the table. His face was wild: 'Now I believe in God! The number of times I've prayed for those thieving buggers to sit down so we can get the lot at once – now my prayer's been answered. I believe in God, I never did before. He's on our side, he's arranged a dinner for us.' With his hands gripped above his head Brunt circled away in a dance of thanksgiving.

'Eight o'clock tomorrow night,' Thistlewood said, calmly but with marvel in his voice. 'Twelve hours after they start their soup the country will be ours.'

'We should sit in committee,' Edwards said. 'I propose Adams for president.'

Adams looked appalled, his crooked face turned into a mask of half death, half horror, and stammered, 'I don't . . . I'm not . . . '

Brunt broke off his dance and accused him: 'You're frightened, that's what,' and thought of something worse: 'What've you heard? You've been to the police.'

Adams said, 'I've got nothing . . . I can't tell you . . . I don't feel well . . . '

'If anyone fails us now,' Ings said, 'or pulls out or doesn't believe . . . '

'I'll run him through,' Harrison said.

'Man, I tell you,' Davidson said, 'we're madmen if we don't see this is our chance.'

Adams said, 'I'm ill today, that's all . . . '

'Let Mr Thistlewood be president,' Edwards proposed.

Thistlewood took the chair at the end of the table. He couldn't hide his pleasure in the simple sense of power and didn't want to. Separate attacks on the ministers' homes would scatter and fail. He had begun to fear that unless he could promise a spectacular success the chance would slip, the men would lose heart and drift away, the shoemakers would try for work, Edwards would find a job, Ings would borrow money and go back to Portsmouth. He said, 'They'll all be there – fourteen of them. It'll be a rare haul. We'll go to Grosvenor Square with fifty men.' Down the table there were less than twenty.

'Be sure it isn't a trap.'

'A decoy.'

'I wouldn't put it past them – a false dinner with false food.'

'For false men.'

'Find out if it's true - if they're getting ready for dinner or if soldiers go in the house.'

'Set a watch on it – two men all tonight and tomorrow till dinner, and anything suspicious, one of them reports it here.'

'Dinner at eight – have it with me tomorrow, you're all invited.'

Thistlewood thumped the table. He was working out a plan, he would share it with the men.

*

. . . I see it as if it has already happened, as if today is the day after tomorrow. It's a memory as much as a prophecy.

We assemble here in the stable with the weapons we can muster. Fifty men at least. We go out in pairs, for safety and not to cause alarm. It's dark in Cato Street, we cross Oxford Street and collect in Grosvenor Square, scattering among the trees. There's no need to talk, we know what to do. I go alone up the steps of number 44 and ring the bell and hear it sounding inside the house – the tocsin for those fourteen men at dinner.

. . . I see the footman's face as he opens the door, pink and keen under a powdered wig. I have a letter for the prime minister. Or better, I have a red dispatch box – Edwards will get it for me. I say it's urgent, it has just arrived and must be delivered immediately. The footman tells me to step into the hall and shuts the door. While he goes to the dining room I wait. Counting to a hundred to give them time outside. They are counting too. Then I open the door and let them in: waiting on the doorstep, fifty of them ready to rush in. Some are masked, all are armed. We seize the servants and threaten to kill them if they shout. But they're on our side, they are the people. We divide. One party takes the staircase, the key to the house. A man can throw a grenade upstairs and take cover before it goes off. The men in front carry a gun in one hand, a sword or pike in the other. If a servant tries to get away we light a grenade to stop him. They understand, they're not our enemies.

. . . I see Davidson on the stairs, and the terror of a housemaid who meets a black man there. Two men are left on guard outside the house, one with a grenade, one with a blunderbuss for anybody escaping by the basement. The assassination party goes straight to the dining room and kills everyone at the table, good or bad. The good must be killed for keeping bad company. But they are all bad.

. . . I see them with their greedy eyes and napkins tucked in, startled at the sight of us as we were startled by Mrs Brunt in the door. A half-eaten cutlet between the teeth, a potato stopped in mid-air, a wine glass raised. One drops a fork on his plate, one chokes, one opens his mouth but no noise comes out except a small pop like a burst bubble. Somebody laughs and Lord Sidmouth catches my eye, the way he did once before. Only he and I know what is happening, we have our own conspiracy. No one else perceives this huge apocalyptic fact of history. Before anyone has time to speak or shout we throw a grenade from the door, take cover while it explodes, then go in and cut them down with swords, if any are left to finish off. Brunt, Harrison, Adams and I have swords – four are enough.

Nobody can touch us now, the moment we get that room. We're astonished how easy it is, and how quick; stunned by our own new power. With one grenade we have killed the cabinet, taken the government of England. All that remains is a spoilt dinner and a smell of gunpowder. A charred tablecloth, some broken glass and blood. The terrified butler and footmen help us to cutlets and wine over the bodies of the ministers, holding silver dishes for us, emptying decanters, mastering their fright and drinking with us to liberty. They are our first recruits, pulling off their wigs and unbuttoning their livery to join us. It doesn't take long, it's simple to undo something that seemed eternal. A possibility stretches out. Five minutes ago it wasn't there; suddenly it has arrived. Everything is so clear, I'm surprised we didn't do it years ago.

We throw fireballs into the other rooms and leave the house. There's a lot of work tonight. Men begin to join immediately, collecting in Grosvenor Square when they hear the grenades and see the flames. First we march to the barracks in Portman Street. Harrison was a soldier there, he knows where the horses are kept and throws a fireball over the wall into the straw. In a moment the building is ablaze, the horses are screaming, the soldiers surrender – or enlist with us. We march to the post in Gray's Inn Road and take the two cannons there, then to the Artillery Ground for six more. Now we're strong enough to attack the Mansion House.

... I see us dragging our cannons through the city and setting them up, loaded and trained on the Mansion House. Cooper is in charge of the guns, I have a megaphone, Edwards can find one. I call on the Mansion House to surrender or we'll open fire and set it alight. Then the Bank of England, the Royal Exchange, Cornhill . . . I see the crowd rushing from Caesar's body. Liberty! Freedom! Tyranny is dead! Rushing down the streets like fire, spreading across London, licking to the suburbs. By Thursday morning we shall have a people's government sitting in the Mansion House, a people's army, a people's treasury.

... I see the effect of another private act like the one when I was a young man in the gallery of parliament. This time I shall change England. Change the world perhaps.

*

From the chimneys round Grosvenor Square smoke rose into the winter afternoon. Nobody lived here who wasn't a lord or bishop or war profiteer: none of them had worries about keeping warm. Behind the railings in the middle of the square some children threw a ball, bowled a hoop, cried sharply across the bare garden. The grass looked thin and grey, the trees incapable of growing leaves. A dog was tied to a seat, barking at the games. Ings thought of his son and three daughters in Portsmouth, walking into the country the way he used to go, to see the animals. And Tidd, who had a daughter, must know what it felt like. Ings studied the tops of the railings: ideal for cannonballs.

A servant from one of the houses told the children it was time to come indoors. They took no notice, didn't even look up. He said it again and they must have heard but went on playing. He turned back to the house, winking at Ings and Tidd – allies, who would understand. Later the children drifted home, leaving their toys and the dog in the empty garden. The servant was sent to fetch them.

Nothing strange was going on at number 44. Somebody went in or came out, or a figure showed at a window, but no more

63

than at other houses: no policemen or soldiers or extra bustle for Ings and Tidd to report when Edwards and Davidson came to relieve them.

The day faded, the lamplighter came round the square. Lights went up in the windows, curtains were drawn. Edwards and Davidson stood in the shadow between two lamps, watching number 44 across the garden. After a while they separated to walk round the square in opposite directions, looking into the basements; passed each other without a word and met again where they had started. By then it was dark. A light flared and died in the corner of the square, from the brazier by the parish watchman's hut. Edwards and Davidson stamped and shivered.

'Tonight's the last,' Davidson said softly. 'Tomorrow night . . . ' He sounded infinitely excited.

Edwards said, 'It'll be quite a dinner party.'

'I'll fetch my blunderbuss from pawn and clean it up. Ten shillings I got. It's a good one – brassbound.'

'You'll find the money?'

'Somewhere.'

'From your wife?'

Davidson laughed: 'Man, she never earned a penny in her life, I'd like to watch her try. All she knows is the way of making babies and she likes it so much she never stops. Come on, Davidson, she says and I'm up and going for another before she's hardly dropped the last.'

'Is she black?'

'White as you.'

'Children?'

'Six, and all of them are hungry.'

'They'll thank you for this.'

'That's besides the ones my wife didn't give me, maybe another six – I never cared to count. All I know is, I don't have to feed them. And all they know is, their father was a black man.'

'You find it's useful?'

'With woman it is. Maybe they hope it's going to be different, as if they feel the colour when it's in.'

'And you don't disappoint them.'

'Being a Sunday school teacher helped. You're one step closer to God, so they think it's right. You get the other teachers

64

and the lonely ones and little girls. After evening church is best, when they've had emotions in there among the candles and don't want to lose them going home in the dark, and you show them how. Another handy thing I found, people can't tell two black men apart. There was a time I was being snubbed though nothing definite was said, so I went to the parish and they told me it was a lady complaining I was taking liberties after church. I acted injured innocence and said the lady was mistaken, and I found another black man to say it was him and he begged her pardon. She couldn't look me in the face, knowing she had accused me wrongly because she couldn't tell the difference and me a Sunday school teacher, so I gave her my hand in God's name and after that – liberties! man, I took them freely but she never saw it was the same who had her after church.' Davidson checked himself, he was talking too much, they might draw attention. But there was nobody moving in the dark square. He asked Edwards, 'You got children?'

'Not married.'

'Too young – leave it a bit.'

'Ten shillings for the blunderbuss, you say – we could get it in the morning. You'll need it.'

They heard the watchman coughing in his box, and his brazier flared again. Davidson said, 'What'll happen when we've killed them?'

'It'll take time,' Edwards said. 'Years, when you see what we're up against.' He looked at the tall houses, invincible and solid in the dark. They grew from deep underground, with rooms below the street where men and women lived in twilit slavery, bleached like animals in the drifting smell of grease and polish and boiled vegetables. Edwards had often seen inside. Tramping London with a box of plaster figures to sell he had climbed down iron stairs, knocked on kitchen doors, stood watching cooks and scullery maids and boot boys turn over his little pieces and say how nice and put them back. Occasionally someone would bargain over the price and with scrubbed and mean old fingers pick out a shilling from a purse. Or his box would be taken to show to the family upstairs while he was kept waiting in the kitchen, but rich people didn't want his stuff, he knew he would be told to go away. Once, in a grand house like these, his box was brought down with one piece missing. None of the servants would go up and complain – to carry his

65

suspicions to the drawing room was to share them, which was
more than they could risk. So they turned on him and accused
him of cheating, and drove him like a dog up to the street. He
remembered the fright in their eyes at the danger they were in,
till they got him out of the house. He could never forgive them.
Their guilt wasn't enough for him: they had betrayed one of
themselves, he would turn their treachery back on them one
day.

Someone walked out of the dark and disappeared. A cat
came from nowhere and rubbed itself on Davidson's legs. A cab
drove into the square, delivered a passenger and drove out. It
began to rain, cold but almost too fine to be felt, hanging like
cobweb over the lamps. The hours passed, told by the chimes
from a church beyond the square, the dwindling traffic, the
watchman's cough. Then Brunt and Adams came to take over
from Edwards and Davidson. The four stood in the dark,
talking in the soft rain.

Adams had had another fright. On the way from Cato Street
with Brunt, crossing Oxford Street, he was shouted at by name.
He didn't dare turn round, but the shock of being recognised
stopped him for an instant before he hurried on. The man
shouted again, then gave a great laugh and swore. Brunt heard
it too and saw the fear in Adams' misshapen face. He pulled
him into a pub and they started arguing. Adams wished Brunt
had never got him mixed up in this, Brunt said whoever
deserted now was as good as dead. There were men in the pub
watching them, Adams was nervous, Brunt didn't care but
became louder and more menacing, ordered more beer and
bread and cheese to show he wasn't afraid, and set up a game of
dominoes with Adams and two strangers. Adams couldn't stop
his pieces rattling on the table, he hated Brunt, he wanted to go
back to find the man who had shouted at him, to get an alibi
and prove he was nothing to do with Brunt. When they came on
watch in Grosvenor Square he wished he had the courage to go
to the watchman's box and surrender.

Edwards tried to calm him: 'It'll be a walkover, you'll see.
Look at them all tucked up in their houses – what could be
easier?'

Brunt said, 'What I was telling him – we could march
through any of those front doors, the fucking four of us, and
they're sitting birds.'

66

Davidson summoned the soothing tropics in his voice: 'Tomorrow we'll be a regiment. By this time of night we'll be on the inside looking out.'

After midnight Thistlewood came striding down the pavement, a tall figure in a blue coat, an officer inspecting his troops. Tomorrow they were going into battle, tonight he could share their vigil, tend their fears, stiffen their courage. His step was confident, bringing authority to Grosvenor Square. As he marched towards them under a lamp they saw the flare of his coat where he carried a sword; shuffled their feet together to salute him and stood a little taller.

'Nothing to report,' Edwards said.

'They don't know what's coming to them,' Brunt said, softened by Thistlewood's presence and the rain.

'Let them be,' Davidson said. 'It's their last night, it'll never be like this again.'

'Remember Brutus and Cassius,' Thistlewood mused. 'They were hailed for killing Caesar.'

Davidson slipped back to the stable in Cato Street, a black man in the night. Brunt and Adams stayed on watch. Thistlewood was restless, he wouldn't sleep but didn't want too many men in the square. He would go for a walk, Edwards could accompany him.

They went through Mayfair together, keeping step and hardly talking. A dog scuttered past, a drunk shouted thickly, a ragged tune came from a concertina. At night the cruelty of London was more tormenting than by day. It taunted a beggar for his poverty; pursued a tramp down the smart streets where he dragged his loneliness.

*

. . . I see it happening on another winter day three years ago. We had arms and ammunition that time too, and two hundred and fifty pikes. I was in charge of the military, I had studied the barracks and talked the soldiers into opening the gates for us. There would be no difficulty, there was enough discontent in the army. We would seize the artillery, barricade the streets and bridges, blow up the post offices and banks, set the prisoners free. I had a plan of the Tower and a list of people for the committee of public safety, like Robespierre's.

. . . I see the crowd on Spa Fields in Islington, thick under

67

the trees, stretching back to the houses. The biggest crowd in my life, the biggest chance to fight for justice. We had banners and tricolour flags and tricolour cockades in our hats. I got up on the wagon and began to shout, with my wife Susan beside me and Julian, our child, and thousands of faces and the feeble winter sun coming out for us. 'Since the Norman conquest the kings and lords have been deceiving us, we're worse off than African slaves – four million are starving but the king and his friends haven't noticed.' Someone passed up a bottle but I didn't need it. I was drunk with my own effort. 'If they don't give us what we want we'll take it.' I jumped down with a flag and we started through the streets – not the whole crowd but enough for what we had to do. Through Clerkenwell and Smithfield to the Royal Exchange, raiding every gunsmith's on the way. A student stole a pistol and shot the man who tried to stop him. The screams roused the people, and when the student was caught we fought our way through and rescued him. But outside the Royal Exchange we met the lord mayor with a squad of police, too strong for us. They took my flag and we scattered. Some of us got away and marched to the Tower where we shouted to the soldiers to join us, but an officer ordered them to shut the gates.

. . . I see now that the crowd was full of Sidmouth's spies. I see the old grub himself, and his contempt. For months I had to lie low with Susan and Julian. There was a price of five hundred pounds for my capture and we moved our lodging every week. But a man can't live in the dark if he's a fighter, a revolutionary. We got a passage to America, the three of us were on board ship in the Thames waiting for the tide when Sidmouth's men came out in a boat to arrest me. The old grub never had to pay the reward, he waited till his agents found me. I wanted Susan to take the boy to America but she wouldn't go, she stayed with me.

. . . I see the clerk of the court reading out the charge – high treason. If Sidmouth had been content with riot he might have got me, but he was greedy. And he cheated. His chief witness was proved to be an informer and the case was discredited. In his summing up the judge did his best for the prosecution but Sidmouth's methods were too vile for an English jury, they acquitted me. Though he suppressed the revolution he never got the conviction he was after.

*

Thistlewood said, 'Well, this looks something like it,' counting thirty men in the loft, some of them strangers. Swords, pistols, muskets everywhere. On the trestle table were grenades and fireballs and ammunition, under it were bundles of pikes. No light came through the sacking over the windows, London was kept out. In the crowded room lit by candles and a lamp nobody cared if it was day or already night. These were the last hours of an era, though only the men here knew it. They threaded string for bootlaces, nailed old files and screwdrivers to pikes, tried their guns, felt the weight, looked down the sights, cleaned out the barrels, tested the flintlocks, sawed and hammered. Edwards had brought a sack of bread and cheese to feed them before going into action and some were squatting in a ring, tearing at the loaves, cutting cheese with a sword. A few had enlisted for the food, but would be grateful and fight the better for it. More weapons were passed up the ladder – a cutlass, the branch of a tree, a broomstick with a stiletto on the end. Gunpowder was measured into flannel bags. There was a smell of tar and sulphur: a limbering up, a last flexing before the show.

Thistlewood put his hand on Adams' shoulder: 'Feeling better?'

Adams winced with half his face: 'A bit low, that's all,' In the afternoon he had been sent out to buy gin and beer. A soldier never went without his weapon and Brunt made him take Davidson's blunderbuss, redeemed from pawn today, under his coat. In Cato Street Adams saw a chance of escape. He had two shillings, he could disappear with that, but never get rid of the blunderbuss. Bloody Brunt – Adams hated him more than ever. With luck he might reach Hyde Park and throw it in the bushes. There was a patch of woodland by the Serpentine where he had often hidden, hoping to turn some easy money. He dodged through an alley into Edgware Road and bumped into Edwards with the sack of food. Adams said he had forgotten something, he was going home for it and anyway was too ill for fighting. Squinting beyond Edwards his single eye picked out the Hyde Park trees at the end of the street. But Edwards saw through him; took him by the elbow and steered him back, stopping at a pub for the gin and beer. This was the day of the revolution, almost the last hour, no time for backing out. Deserters were as bad as traitors. In the stable he told Thistlewood that Adams must be watched.

Thistlewood pressed his fingers into Adams' shoulder: 'You were in the Life Guards?'

'The Blues.'

'You'll be one of the swordsmen for the dining room.'

'You'll need another drink,' Brunt said, pouring more gin for Adams. 'It'll be cold out there tonight.'

Tidd said, 'Warm enough in Grosvenor Square.'

'Drink will do us no good,' Davidson warned them, polishing his blunderbuss. But Thistlewood told Brunt to get another bottle, also some cardboard for placards. Adams wasn't let out again, Tidd was sent.

Little Ings was ready for battle: a haversack over his shoulder, two belts for a pair of pistols and a cutlass. The cutlass belonged to his wife's family, he would avenge them with it. He had had it ground and pointed in Smithfield – a good job done, though he felt an idiot walking through the market with a cutlass. He had sharpened his butcher's knife too and bound the handle with wax and tape for a better grip. He ran his finger down the blade, thinking of more than meat.

When Tidd brought the cardboard Thistlewood and Edwards cleared space among the bombs on the table. Elegantly Edwards traced, '*Proclamation to the Inhabitants of the Metropolis! Your Tyrants have been Destroyed!*' Thistlewood's hands trembled, he was too excited to write: 'We'll put them up near the fires we start, so they can be read by the flames. And more for the barracks.' The men watched Edwards' huge letters appear: '*Join the Friends of Liberty! Fight for Freedom! Every Man is offered his Discharge and Twenty Pounds to get him Home!*'

'I'll be first in the dining room,' Ings cried, striking a pose with his butcher's knife, the cutlass and pistols hanging from his waist. 'I'll stand at the door – "Well, my lords, I've got as good men behind me as any in the kingdom! Enter, citizens, and do your duty!"'

'The grenade first,' Brunt said, 'then go in and cut them up.'

Ings grabbed a sack off the floor: 'It'll hold a couple of heads – Sidmouth's . . . ' He swiped the air with his knife. 'And Castlereagh's.' He swiped again. 'I'll take them home and pickle them and one day sell them for my family – they'll be worth something.'

The men watched, listened, muttered in the shadows of the loft.

'Hope you know what we're up to.'

'What am I expected to do? – I've never been a soldier.'

'Give us the plan.'

'If you don't like it or you're afraid, quit and let the rest get on without.'

'And see the way you've thrown away your chance.'

'How does killing the cabinet help?'

'How d'you know the people will join when it's been done?'

'Man, I tell you, you're pouring cold water on it.'

'No time for doubts – you'll know what you have to do when you have to do it and anyone who deserts, I'll fucking kill him.'

'We haven't got the men.'

'Trust Mr Thistlewood! – look what he's done for us.' Brunt swept his big hands over the weapons, ammunition, bread, cheese, beer: 'This is a start and now you'll be free to help yourselves.'

Thistlewood's voice quelled them: 'However many servants, they'll surrender as soon as we come in, they won't be ready. We could do it with half this number.'

'For every one of us,' Brunt boasted, 'there are ten outside.'

'More like a hundred,' Edwards said, catching the theme.

'Like missionaries,' Davidson said. 'We'll make converts on the way.' With his gleaming blunderbuss he defied the doubters – a smart black soldier wearing a white belt with shoulder straps.

'Pick them out of the pubs.'

'Call them from the flats.'

'They're waiting for the signal, they mustn't be let down.'

'Keep watch till the end.'

'Dinner at eight.'

'I could do it on my own,' Tidd shouted – the timid, bald shoemaker blushing at his own belligerence. 'Sooner than give up, I'd blow up the dinner myself – anyone could, with any courage.'

'Put yourselves under Mr Thistlewood,' Edwards ordered. 'He's commander.'

Thistlewood protested: 'We're equal, I don't hold rank above you. But don't forget what we're here for – there are

71

bigger things above us all.'

'Ten minutes to Grosvenor Square!' Brunt roared.

Harrison said, 'On watch I saw a grocer's van . . . '

'Poultry and meat and onions being taken in,' Cooper added.

'This is history,' Thistlewood said, too exultant to speak of responsibility, liberty, change.

Edwards gave him a glass of gin, emptying the bottle. Ings and Davidson went down to the stable, as sentries. Edwards said, 'I'll fetch more to drink – there's the Horse and Groom at the corner.' He too went down the ladder.

*

. . . I see the face of my watch, but can't read the time. My eyes are going, soon I shall be old. I hold it to a candle: a quarter past eight. They're sitting at the table, the footmen are clearing away the soup, the prime minister is speaking for the last time.

. . . I see the minute hand slipping off the quarter. Time for us to go. Ten minutes to Grosvenor Square, Brunt said – to the revolution. At half past eight we shall be there. I put the watch in my pocket and take out my snuff-box. I wish I could stop this tremble.

. . . I see the faces of the men when they hear the noise. Unbelieving, frightened, accusing me. Down in the stable under us. I know exactly what it is. A heavy thud as if something has hit the foundations, then a voice. It isn't the sentries, Ings or Davidson. A voice coming from under the floor, rising through the cracks and knot-holes, filling the loft, commanding anyone it reaches. The voice of the past and future coming up from below. I feel I'm sinking into it . . . I see the scaffold in the square, the houses, the people in front.

'Hello there, show a light!'

I take a candle to the top of the ladder but the flame dazzles me, I can't see down. My weakening eyes. An old man soon. *Soon* . . . I see my hand shaking. The men see it too. They know there's nothing I can do for them, they must save themselves. I put the candle on the table. Now there are steps on the ladder, boots coming up. The floor trembles.

From the stable Ings shouts up, 'Men!'

Davidson shouts, 'Look out above!' before his voice is stifled. A mighty blow down in the stable, and cries. Someone drops a sword, the boots come up the ladder. I fall back into the shadow among the men against the wall, waiting for whoever it is, it doesn't matter who . . . I see my sword on the table. Jump forward, grab it, pull it from the scabbard – a long bright blade. I fall back again. A tall hat, black beard, high collar – a policeman on the ladder, rising through the hatch. Another behind him, a third pushing from below. Coming up like the dark sea into a sinking ship. The lurching floor. My life is tilting, it will slip away under the surface of the world. Uniforms, buttons, red winter faces, truncheons, pistols. They're fighting down there, Ings is shouting, Davidson trumpeting like an elephant.

The policeman steps off the ladder: 'Hello, here's a pretty nest!'

'Holy fucking Christ!'

'The password!'

'Gentlemen, we have a warrant for your arrest.' He looks at me. We've met before, years ago. It's ridiculous – two men together again, one with a sword, one with a pistol. A funny coincidence, a mutual surprise to exchange in a loft above a stable. A joke to share on this black night of treachery. A pretty nest, he calls it. A table between us, laden with weapons. 'We hope you'll come peacefully.'

Two policemen sweep their pistol muzzles over us. One lifts his truncheon, one is pushed up the ladder from below.

'Take their weapons!'

'Surrender!'

'Make way – let me come up!' A fourth policeman on the ladder.

. . . I see myself in the middle of my men, a cornered animal snarling, teeth bared, heart knocking in my chest and neck and head. The men shrink away to leave me alone with my sword. Shaking the blade at the policemen, fencing. I am famous for my swordsmanship

'Kill the buggers!' After the first seconds of astonishment the men spring. A clattering of guns, rattling of steel, shouts and oaths.

'Throw them out!'

'Down the ladder!'

My arm goes out with the sword.

'Drop it or I'll fire!' A policeman's arm with a pistol.

'Make way!' Another policeman lunges forward to take me.

73

Handcuffs, a rope . . . I see a rope in his hands. A hangman's weapon, not a soldier's. I rush at him. A long bright sword, a pistol – the sword gets there first. It shoots out faster than a pistol ball, punctures the uniform which bursts. I pull the blade out, blood spurts after it, ejected from a living body. I must have touched the heart. The pump in my own body, racing for my life.

'Oh God, I'm done, oh . . . ' The uniform folds up, collapses on the floor. A terrific bump – he was a heavy man. The wooden loft shudders. Brunt swipes a pike at the lamp, smashing it. It expires before the wounded policeman. The tinkling innocent glass. Someone throws a hat, punches a fist, kicks out a foot, lashes with a cutlass and in a moment ten candles are snuffed. The lights are out, the last flash is from a policeman's pistol, but the ball goes past me.

'I'm done, oh God.' Someone dies in the dark. I killed him . . . I see him a moment ago, coming at me with a rope. Utmost confusion after the lights go out, thick and dangerous. Shots, shouts, a scrum of blows and grapples. Arms and gun barrels and sticks swinging. Someone overturns the table, grenades and fireballs are tipped on the floor, rolling between my feet. One of them will explode.

'Down the ladder with the buggers!'

A rush to the ladder, Brunt leading. A policeman in the hatch is knocked to the bottom without touching the steps. Others fall on top of him, a tumble of men to the ground.

'Kill them!'

Boots in men's faces, hats knocked off, swords catching in the ladder, teeth clenched for a yell or a hiss or a rattle.

'Get them!'

Police and plotters in the dark. Anybody's an enemy, everybody's in the way. To get out is the thing, to escape. A man screams, a man starts hitting wildly everywhere. Bruises, blood, shots behind my neck, explosions in my face. The loft is packed with smoke, noise, arms. A man tears the sacks off the window, smashes the panes, pokes his gun out, firing into the street at random. Another pulls him aside and jumps through the window. Bolting in all directions. It's the only thing. A man climbs up on the rafters to break the slates. Others follow . . . I see the sky through a hole in the roof. The night comes in.

I fall over something on the floor at the top of the ladder. The policeman I killed. I kick something else – a pistol. Pick it up and in a single bound I'm down the ladder. No longer an old man suddenly, but strong and alert, a fighter with my sword and pistol. There's more light down here in the stable . . . I see little Ings fighting a policeman in one of the stalls. The policeman knocks the butcher's knife from his hand, Ings reaches for his cutlass, sharpened in Smithfield for this. More men fall down the ladder, an avalanche. Ings jumps for the stable door, the policeman gets him by the collar, I go for the policeman and stab him in the thigh with the point of my sword. Davidson is fighting another policeman, cutlass and pistol in his belt, a sword in one hand, the blunderbuss in the other. The policeman holds him round the neck, screws his head.

'A nigger!'
'Get him.'
'Where are the soldiers?'
'Stop him!'
'Fuck the soldiers.'

Davidson breaks free and rushes for the street, a wild beast with two policemen after him. But the black man is weighed down with weapons, tamed too easily. He screams, then weeps. They have him, they're binding him . . . I see his misery. He cries, 'Fight on, fight on while you've got blood in you, you may as well die now.' Then weeps again, the terrible misery of a black man, a primitive howl from the jungle . . . I see Robespierre on the scaffold. The executioner pulling the bandage off his broken jaw, his mouth falling open for a hideous cry.

. . . I see Tidd lifting his gun to fire. Two policemen twist him by the arms, all three fall together, the pistol goes off, but Tidd is secured. They rip his belt off, tie his hands with it, tear away his coat, rip open the pockets. Balls and cartridges fall out on the brick floor, stamped and soiled by horses. The policemen pounce like clumsy cats, grabbing and missing.

I make a cut at a policeman but there are men everywhere, I'm jogged and only slash his hand. He comes at me again, we close. I put my pistol to his head, he throws up his hand to knock it away, I fire, the ball goes through his hat, he rushes at me, I catch him on the jaw with the muzzle, then leap for the stable door, cutting at everybody in the way.

75

'Get him!'

'I am a magistrate, I am a magistrate . . . ' A man waving a piece of paper outside the stable.

They follow me . . . I see the street and men running . . . I see the Paris cobbles flying under my feet, Clothilde pulling my hand. People are at the windows and doors. And now soldiers. Fuck the soldiers, they're on the wrong side. Fuck Clothilde too. *Join the Friends of Liberty! Fight for Freedom!* A squad of guards with a sergeant. An absurd officer under a lamp trying to read something. He has lost his way, he doesn't know this street, he has forgotten his orders. I run past but he doesn't see me. I have never run like this. My legs are weakening like my eyes, soon I shall be an old man. Fighting all up the street . . . I see Adams running towards the soldiers with his hands up: 'Murder, murder! There's been a plot!' Fleeing to save his skin, switching sides already. I would drive my sword into him if I could reach. But the soldiers came too late, they're eager to make up for it, they must show their bravery. I run through them, my sword in front like a ship's bowsprit. A long bright blade, now with blood on it. Two soldiers catch a policeman and stick their bayonets into him, then see who it is, drop him and catch little Ings instead. I thought he had got away. A pistol shot explodes close to him, but I'm running, running . . . I see Edwards in the street ahead.

'I killed a policeman,' I shout to him.

We're running together, Edwards and I. Out of Cato Street, side by side. Clothilde and I. I don't know where we're running to. Edwards and Clothilde and I . . . I see Edgware Road in front.

*

Hobhouse shivered on a bench in the parlour of the Horse and Groom, hunched by the fire in a monstrous dirty greatcoat from Bow Street police station. He crossed and uncrossed his legs under its skirts as if friction could conjure a little warmth; pushed his hands up and down the sleeves, rubbed and craned his neck inside the filthy collar. If it wasn't alive with fleas when he borrowed it, it would have picked them up here.

This wasn't a thing he liked, but he could extract a thin cold pleasure from the irony. He had been in pubs before and this was the dingiest. The brandy was undrinkable – thank God he had brought his own. A crested silver flask stood on the table beside the glass of poison put there by the landlord, which smelt so powerful that Hobhouse hadn't touched it. The jug of water also looked unsafe. He was content to drink straight from his flask, though it had been in the pocket of the disgusting coat. Good brandy couldn't bring much cheer to this chilly little hole, but it was a link with a familiar world and helped Hobhouse's peculiar sense of indulgence. In his way he was gratified to be here.

Without having seen any conspirators tonight, apart from George, he had at least heard some of their voices. An hour or so ago, from behind the parlour door, he listened while a man in the bar ordered a gallon of beer and half a pint of gin to take away. Hobhouse felt the nearest thing to a thrill at being so close to drama and violence – a distaste that was oddly enjoyable. Later, when two more came in for beer and he heard them talking in the next room, he tingled with delight not just in the power behind him but in the unexpected turns of a plan which could still be affected by the curious minds and motives of other men. Satisfied that nothing could alter the final result, he didn't mind a few small changes before the end.

The potboy, who had been given a shilling by George, had brought information that was hardly vital though Hobhouse was glad to have it. This afternoon the boy had seen a small man hurrying under the archway at the end of the street with a sack over his shoulder and a parcel partly hidden by his butcher's apron. At dusk the boy had been sent with a bottle of spirits to a house where a woman had fainted after seeing a sword under the coat of a black man who had come to her door with ten candles, asking for a light. On his way back to the Horse and Groom the boy had watched men going into a stable which was known to be unoccupied. He heard someone shout but the windows were sealed, the noise was muffled. Just now the boy had brought in something left by the two men in the bar, a thing like a mop handle with a rusty knife tied to the end.

The shooting couldn't be heard in the parlour. The first Hobhouse knew of the attack was a prisoner being brought in: Tidd, who had been taken in the stable without a fight. For the shoemaker the sight of police evoked the old vision of the scaffold, his new courage vanished, he surrendered as if it would be cheating to be killed by a sword or pistol. Next was

Davidson: a scuffle outside the parlour and a bellow, half song, half shout, 'Scots wha hae wi' Wallace bled!' ending in a scream, 'Liberty's in every blow! Let us do or die!' Hobhouse hadn't heard the highland words from a black man's lips before. The police clapped handcuffs on him and told him to shut up.

Then Ings was hustled in. He had been fleeing with Thistlewood when the picket arrived, and wriggled out of their hands and ran on. With high hats and boots and muskets the soldiers couldn't catch him, but a policeman chased him down the street. Ings turned and fired his pistol, the policeman lurched to the ground, hit in the shoulder. When Ings aimed the second shot it misfired. The policeman got up and chased again, shouting for help. In the next street a night watchman stepped out with a stick in front of Ings who threw his empty pistol at him, missed, then suddenly stopped. He would give himself up, he was winded, appalled at what he could already see ahead. The watchman got him by a wrist and beat his knuckles till they bled, though Ings put up no fight. The policeman called him a bastard to shoot at a stranger, and Ings said he had fired to kill, he wished he had, he knew what was coming to him. In the Horse and Groom, handcuffed and disarmed, he was no longer the fierce little ruffian of an hour ago, he had shrunk with fear, his fiery eyes burnt out. He was used to blood on his hands but never a man's blood before, never his own. In horror he wondered if his memory was right: he had begged the policeman not to kill him, he would tell everything to be spared.

More were brought into the Horse and Groom, stunned, wounded, in despair. Cooper the sailor who was to command the artillery, Bradburn who once brought a bundle of pikes to Fox Court, Harrison who had survived the cavalry charge on St Peter's Fields, and Wilson, Gilchrist, Strange – nine had been caught, for one policeman killed. They were stripped and assembled against the wall, outnumbered by police; their coats torn off, pockets turned out. Wilson had twenty cartridges, a flint, a pair of scissors. Bradburn had a bag of pistol balls but no pistol, Harrison a tin of gunpowder, Strange a broken dagger, Gilchrist a penknife in a fancy case and a box of fuses, Cooper a handful of slugs. Davidson opened his mouth for another bellow and got as far as 'By oppression's woes and pains!'

before being kicked on the shins. Tidd asked for someone to vouch that he had surrendered without resisting and got punched in the stomach. Ings, reaching to his waistcoat pocket, was slapped across the face. Belts and braces were pulled off, pieces of string and scarves taken from them. The cheeky potboy, bringing mugs of beer for the police, grinned at the prisoners. Everyone ignored the man on a bench in a grubby coat, drinking from a silver flask.

The captain of the picket came into the parlour, a young man with weak blue eyes floating behind soft hair like a silly dog returning from an escapade. Conscious of having arrived late, he could blame the police for arriving early. It was a matter of bluff. He affected a limp crossing the room and a wince sitting down, then called to his sergeant to send in a bottle of claret if one could be found in such a hovel, and arranged his scarlet uniform so that anyone could see how the sleeve was torn. Nobody but the sergeant knew that the picket was late because the captain couldn't be found. Nobody but the captain knew that it was because he was in bed with a whore, having trouble with his erection; or that in Cato Street he had seen a wild man with a sword, unmistakably the famous duellist, running from the stable, but had tackled an unarmed cobbler instead; or that nothing had frightened him so much as tripping over a corpse into a pile of bombs. The only comfort was that he got the dead man's blood on his white breeches and a bruise on his hip, and when he was back with the whore tonight, fresh from battle, she might coax him into better shape. Till then a bottle of claret was the least he had earned.

Hobhouse's flask was empty. The prisoners would be chained and marched off to Bow Street, and in time he would see them all again. The soldiers were the property of another ministry, he could dismiss them from his cares. Somehow he must report to Lord Sidmouth that Thistlewood and many others had slipped away, but convince him that they would be caught within twenty-four hours. A reward might be offered, a thousand pounds would do. But there was George to think of. To allow an agent to claim a reward was something new. It might be dangerous, it might be rather clever: Hobhouse considered it, making his way through dark unsavoury streets to Oxford Street. He would get a cab. Or two cabs – one to take him to Whitehall, one to take the disgusting greatcoat back to Bow Street.

*

. . . I see the morning through the gaps in the shutters. By the light and traffic it must be ten o'clock. I have been sleeping twelve hours. Half awake, I'm aware of people moving on the stairs outside my room. But it isn't mine . . . I see unfamiliar furniture, a strange bed I'm lying on, a room I don't know. My blue coat hanging up, but nothing else of mine. I have never lain under this ceiling. Trousers and socks still on me – I didn't undress last night. Straight to sleep after all the nights without it. In a moment I shall remember where I am.

. . . I see Edwards and myself coming here together. We stopped running, and walked fast down Oxford Street and through Holborn. It wouldn't be safe to go home, I had been seen and there would be a search. Edwards knew a house in the Barbican he had lodged in, where nobody would ask questions – thank God for Edwards . . . I see the name on the corner, Whitecross Street, Little Moorfields. We didn't talk much. Edwards said someone had given us away, they wouldn't have come with so many police and soldiers if they hadn't known. I was curiously unworried, surprised at my own calm – perhaps it was having Edwards with me. I could save myself, all I needed was a place to go to. He brought me here and left me, we must separate. Find a ship to the Channel Islands, Ireland, anywhere. Easy to get abroad, to America or South Africa, any ship would take me – a word with the captain and a few pounds. Edwards can find the money. None of my own left, everything was spent on the revolution, not a farthing to my name. Good timing, to begin again with nothing. A sort of rightness, justice. But I shall need something to get me away, to board a ship in the Thames like before. Leave Susan and Julian behind this time, to follow later when I'm settled. Edwards spoke of friends in Holland where he can disappear, and I might go first to France. There's always the Hôtel de Moscovie in Paris . . . I see Clothilde welcoming me, showing me a room. She still can't pronounce my name.

. . . I see the light under the door, stirred by shadows. People are moving outside it. I locked it after Edwards left and put the key in my coat pocket. My blue coat with velvet collar, hanging on a hook, the pockets sagging with pistol balls. I threw the pistol over a wall in Holborn with my sword. I wanted to keep the sword but Edwards said it must go. The long bright blade . . . I see the fountain of blood from the policeman's chest, from the pressure inside. The point went through to the back ribs. Dead in thirty seconds – I wish it was Sidmouth.

Men on the stairs, going off to work. The landlady's voice, the sound of keys unlocking cupboards. Someone walking in the room above, across the ceiling. I will stay an hour or two till the house is empty, then get up and leave . . . I see Clothilde, in a flash, telling me of Robespierre's arrest. I was in parliament when he made his last speech from the tribune, pale with ill health and foreboding. His voice turned raucous as it cut and lashed and denounced, but mutiny was growling in the chamber, nobody listened to him any more. He could call for the traitors to be arrested, for death and still more death, but never imprison the omens or guillotine the clouds . . . I see froth on his grey lips as he spat the bitter words, claiming woes and virtues for himself and his readiness to die. But when he stepped down there was an evil silence, a hollow in the air. Not a breath or flicker from the gallery. Like the moment after death – a suspension of other men's lives for the passing of one man's, before they continued without him. He wouldn't be missed, nobody would notice the empty space he had filled. The same would happen to the others one day, it was the only certainty. The greatest orator of all had slipped away, incredulous at the speed of cruelty, the quick descent. Slipped into apathy, uncaring. Clothilde said that when they came to take him he didn't lift a finger to save himself, lifting my own to touch it with her tongue.

. . . I see the door opening at last. I knew it would happen, I couldn't wait much longer. The landlady must have given them a key but I never heard it in the lock. Softly opening. They have reason to be cautious, I killed one of them last night. I lie still, I shall lie here for ever, till the end. My heart has stopped, I am in a tomb. This is what it's like – on my back, arms beside me, deadly cold. The door is half open . . . I see the muzzle of a pistol caught in a crack of light from the shutters, then a truncheon, then a policeman. I lift my head from the pillow and look at him. He won't shoot, I know. We have met before somewhere, years ago, and again in the loft last night. An old friend with a warrant for my arrest –I'm sorry for him and I think he sees it. He holds me in his eyes, beckoning with his truncheon to three more policemen who rush from behind him and jump on me.

Three men on top. I don't know what they want, they don't know either. Not to kill me, not to let me live. One kneels on my shoulders and pins my arms, one pulls away the blankets, one sits on my knees and holds my ankles. The bed can't support us, it crumples to the floor. The fools, they can't see I won't resist, they only break someone's furniture. Tear the bedding and mattress apart, open drawers, looking for something that isn't there. They turn out my coat pockets and the pistol balls roll out with some flints and cartridges. They take my belt and a silk sash I once bought in Paris, then tell me to get dressed. It doesn't take long, my trousers and socks are already on. One of them has his pistol on me. They want to make sure of my humiliation, but I feel only tired and impatient.

With my blue coat on I'm told to hold out my wrists for handcuffs. The pinched skin and sense of helpless bondage as they're clipped shut. Out to the landing, down the stairs. People of the household stand at their doors to watch us pass, the landlady wrings her apron – nobody has been escorted from her house before. In the street a crowd has collected with policemen everywhere. Someone shouts, 'Hang him!' and the rest join in. A policeman lifts his truncheon and they stop. 'Make way!' They stand back for me, I am untouchable or infectious. A jeer, a hoot, a laugh – I'm sitting with four policemen in a cab. They pull down the blinds and tell me to sit back in the seat.

On the way to Bow Street they say that Brunt was taken this morning at Fox Court. Nine were caught last night in Cato Street, eleven in all. I shall see them soon. Brunt must have gone home, believing he hadn't been noticed in the muddle, pleased with himself . . . I see him getting back to his wife, blustering in with his dirty boots and scowl, telling his daughter to brush his clothes, clearing away any evidence in the little back room . . . I see him standing on Ings' bed to hang his wife's red apron over the window, and the black saucepan on the fire, months ago.

Stepping from the cab, escorted into the police station, I catch a heavy blow on the back of my neck. Half stunned, I feel suddenly sick. It's a police officer behind me, using the side of his fist – for the policeman killed last night, a friend of his. I tell him I'm surprised an officer should hit a prisoner from behind, he wouldn't do it if I wasn't in handcuffs, and walk on.

. . . I see the routine before it happens, I have been through it often. The questioning, the laborious copying into a book of height and weight, colour of hair and eyes and complexion, location of scars or peculiar marks. Then the rough inspection, stripping and examining my clothes, big hands behind my ears, in my armpits, between my legs . . . I see, suddenly from the past, a time when six of us were arrested and an officer, with his hat off and a touch of gallantry, apologised for an inconvenience – at night we must be secured with a light chain. He was so polite, we were happy to consent, and sang and ate and talked and slept, chained together and to our beds.

*

Sidmouth delighted in the details: a meticulous care for shoelaces, fingernails, nostrils, earholes. While surveying the wide issues, watching the main policies, he noted the little things. Some of his pleasure could be shared with Hobhouse: since Lady Sidmouth's death there was nobody else. Soon he would call the secretary in, but first he must make a short entry in the journal. A point had come to him today which shouldn't escape his biographer.

It had pleased him to have the eleven prisoners brought to Whitehall to be examined by the cabinet; he hoped it had pleased his colleagues. It wasn't the usual practice but this was an extraordinary occasion. With the ministers seated round a polished table the resemblance to a dinner party wasn't lost. Even such debased mortals must have been struck by the depth of their plight. For humanity's sake Sidmouth told Hobhouse to have them shaved and given food and a pint of beer each. They were lined up in his office, handcuffed in pairs, except Thistlewood who was put to stand in front of the others.

They looked a sorry gang but despite their poverty, pathetic clothes and bandages and black eyes, they failed to show the abject ignominy which Sidmouth had promised himself. They were told that they were charged with high treason, Thistlewood with murder too, and asked if they had any answer, but when each declined it was from scorn, not shame.

Sullen defiance was visible particularly in Thistlewood.

Sidmouth remembered him described as strong and active, and imagined him like a seafaring man. Now he was thin, hardly filling his clothes, but although the minister would have liked the face to be marked by dejection and the terror pitiful to see, it wasn't so. When Thistlewood requested a pen and paper in his cell and permission to keep a diary, Sidmouth advised the cabinet that it was normally not granted to a state prisoner and their painful duty was to refuse. Thistlewood's slow brown eyes, to Sidmouth so malign and contemptible, drifted round the room with disdain, not fear, and when they settled for a baleful moment on the ministers it wasn't Thistlewood who looked uneasy. Under questioning he was proud, indifferent, enigmatic, a symptom of the times, a lamentable product of modern education. That was the trouble: too much education. Schools were being built all over the place now, it was a wonder where the money came from.

Thinking of it again, alone at his desk, Sidmouth allowed his fingers to reach for the drawer and his lips to form a paragraph for the journal: '*Never in his career had he been an admirer of universal education. It was dangerous as well as unkind to provide highly-cultivated talent beyond the country's needs because the surplus was likely to turn sour. That was the truth behind half the reformers and revolutionaries who plagued England . . .*' But he was in no mood to make a speech. It had been a shock to see Thistlewood, he couldn't forget him. On being dismissed the man had led his friends briskly from the room and outside the door had bounded down a flight of stairs. It was a long time since Sidmouth had been so agile, even without handcuffs. But that wasn't a detail to share with Hobhouse.

He rang the silver bell and, when the secretary came in, said, 'Bravery must be rewarded, Hobhouse – we'll open a subscription for the police. I shall start it with a pound, to encourage the public.'

The minister's courage in the face of so desperate an atrocity had been acknowledged in letters from friends and strangers. One or two came from the working class, which was a special comfort: as long as the character of English gentlemen remained what it was, the mob would never succeed in a revolution. They could shout and bang sticks and throw bottles, but this would always be the country where virtue triumphed over vice, loyalty over rebellion. Reports came in from everywhere denouncing the plot as the most depraved to have entered the human imagination, ringing with horror at the infamy which these creatures had brought to England. Minds were staggered, differences of class and party forgotten in the united indignation. But though it was heartening to be supported by the lowliest in the land, the congratulations which most gratified Sidmouth came from Brighton, where the king had gone to recover from his shock. In his gracious note he said, 'You are the Duke of Wellington on home service,' and Sidmouth knew at once that the stories of his colleague's private life were false. The king wasn't strong enough to return for the celebration in St Paul's when the cabinet gave thanks for God's mercy and their own survival, but from the pulpit the Archbishop of Canterbury told them that he had driven down to Brighton with his sermon for approval. The royal message he brought back was of praise for the government's vigour in detecting a crime which nearly brought England to a condition unknown except in France. The devil, in ambush throughout the country, had been trounced again by ministers who had saved themselves only to save the kingdom. If England was to be preserved as England, if Christian men were to be spared the sight of their property set on fire and the sound of terrorists outside their windows, it was the king's conviction – with the help of God and the archbishop – that this cabinet alone could do it.

The music of such words echoed for days in a grateful, loyal old politician's ear and filled his shrivelled heart with generosity. He said to Hobhouse, 'We'll pay for the policeman's funeral.'

The secretary turned over his papers: 'I have the surgeon's evidence at the inquest. He found a wound under the right breast two inches long, half an inch broad, twelve inches deep. The membranes could only have been severed by a very sharp instrument which entered between the fifth and sixth ribs, touched the right lobe of the liver, passed through the diaphragm, lacerated the pericardium and the right ventricle of the heart, penetrated the left lobe of the lungs, struck . . .'

'Thank you, Hobhouse.' Sidmouth was thinking what he had missed when he declined Thistlewood's challenge to a duel. 'Murder is against God's commandment and I see no difficulty in getting our verdict on that count, but where there's

85

a more serious charge . . . ' He closed his eyes briefly for a better view of treason and its consequences, then remembered that his own heart had been touched not by a sword but by charity: 'We'll grant a pension to the policeman's widow – I think a hundred pounds is right.'

'And George . . . '

'Ah, George – I'm glad you mentioned George.'

'He'll be in danger, we can't use him again.'

'There must be a proper gratuity, of course. I'll consider it – a passage to America perhaps, or South Africa, and the title to a small property.'

*

Life in Newgate was a pattern of certainty and suspense. Days and nights, monotony and repetition, misery and boredom stretched backwards and forwards without limit, seldom marked by anything that wasn't the same. Even the unexpected grew into the familiar, so that small surprises – a door opening at an irregular time, a carrot among the potatoes in the soup, a fresh face appearing or an old one leaving – were lost in the overbearing pressure of routine. A thousand men, locked into each other's lives, were imprisoned in a sense of such helplessness that an order from a guard or the jingle of a key inside the walls could become as unreal as the sound of traffic or a church bell outside. The novelty of one man's privilege or another's penalty was absorbed into everyone's punishment: the accumulation of meals, duties, interviews, periods of exercise, wastes of futility, the eternal business of it all – the clanging of gates and banging of locks and rattling of commands.

But somehow, though little leaked out, much seeped in. A new prisoner arrived, another had a visitor, a third got a quick look at a guard's newspaper. News came of crimes, trials, verdicts, sentences, executions, releases, more crimes. The king, back in London for his birthday after recovering from the Cato Street affair, was given a double salute of guns and the public were given a holiday. At the elections the government was returned with a few seats lost, not to the opposition who campaigned mostly in country houses and hunting-fields, but to a handful of unknown radicals. The stock exchange rallied at the election news, the king drove in state to open the new parliament and a cabinet was formed with the same ministers as before. Only a small minority of the people had a vote, and some of the rest showed their annoyance by attacking the houses of ministers and their friends. A military force was sent to suppress the troubles in Yorkshire and Lancashire and preserve the peace up there. The king had a cold which settled on his lungs, and prayers went up from the hearts of all his people. In Manchester the trial of the criminals taken at St Peter's Fields ended in long prison sentences for them all. The magistrates of Glasgow, alarmed by idle workers in the streets and unconcerned whether they were on strike or unemployed or provoked by radicals, scattered them with a battalion of riflemen supported by artillery and cavalry. One marchioness succeeded another in the king's bed, and the queen's name was removed from the prayer book. Notices went up at night proclaiming that equality was the object of the coming struggle. The Russian embassy closed its shutters for fear of broken glass. A man in a pub was arrested for saying he would sooner shoot the king than Thistlewood, and a party of revellers was beaten up by soldiers for drinking seditious toasts and saying that priests and politicians should be flayed and their skins stretched on the drums of the new republican army. Two utterers of forged notes, two servants who had robbed their masters, a horse thief and a cattle thief were hanged in one day. Seventy-seven others were under sentence of death and though the king had power of reprieve, which he found easier to exercise after a dose of laudanum, Lord Sidmouth warned him of the danger if any were only transported to Australia. In Scotland a gang of bandits with pikes and pistols were stopped by a squadron of cavalry who wounded several and took nineteen prisoners for the loss of one horse killed. In Ireland terrorists of the Riband Brotherhood continued their attacks on people and property, breaking into gentlemen's houses to plunder and kill. A form of oath for a novice brother was found on one of them, swearing that he wasn't a protestant or freemason, that he would suffer gibbeting and dissection before informing against another brother, that he wouldn't see a brother go short of sixpence or a meal or a night's lodging, or watch a brother struck in public without going to his aid, or have carnal knowledge of a brother's wife or sister or daughter except in the way of matrimony, or buy anything from a protestant unless he could get it cheaper or better than from a catholic, and that he would have nothing to do with the king or his men unless poverty compelled him. In Cuba, a Spanish colony, it was reported that more than two thousand slaves passed through the Havana customs each month. In France a young lady died of cancer after cleaning out her ears with a brass pin. In Kent, for a bet of twenty guineas, an athlete undertook to run half a mile in two minutes and ten miles in an hour. At Ipswich workers rioted when their demand for half-a-crown a day was refused. At a banquet the lord mayor of London said that if the French nobles had learnt to play cricket with the peasants their châteaux would never have been burnt. When the Duke of Wellington was presented to a pensioner aged a hundred who had fought at Culloden in 1745 and lost an eye at Brandywine in the American war, he shook the old soldier's hand and further honoured him with a pound note. The price of bread had gone up four times since the war, and taxes ten times. A bookseller who published a parody of the Church of England was accused of ridiculing the chief source of human happiness and improvement, and put on trial for blasphemy; but the judge, who was blind and dying of gout, so confused the jury with his muddle between a godfearing Christian and a bloodstained Jacobin that they decided the bookseller's crime was political, not religious, and acquitted him. In a debate on the use of spies and informers parliament showed its confidence in the cabinet by a majority of three to one. The prime minister said that he had nothing against catholics except their religion, that popery was opposed to the progress of knowledge, and that the Church of England had evolved from a dread of arbitrary power but the Church of Rome was the instrument of despotism, if not the devil.

Like a sponge the prison soaked up any items it could collect, and retained them long after they were forgotten outside. To prisoners the stale was still topical, the unimportant significant, the trivial treasured, and time was measured in touches of the season that pricked more sharply than usual. From the earlier dawns stealing into a cell and the brighter afternoons hanging in the patch of sky above the yard, from a bit of fluff in a sparrow's beak or tiny changes of moisture on a wall or the barest thaw noticeable only to a man expert in degrees of frost, it was felt – for in Newgate observation was mainly feeling – that the coldest winter in memory was melting into a wet spring.

During March and April, by chance or through the governor, news reached Thistlewood and his companions that
affected their agonising uncertainty. They were to be charged
under a statute five hundred years old and a lawyer had offered
to defend them without fee. One of the new radicals in
parliament asked Lord Sidmouth for a man called George
Edwards to be charged also, but the minister replied that there
were insufficient grounds and anyway Edwards couldn't be
traced. A shoemaker called Adams surrendered, claiming to be
one of the conspirators, and after four days in Bow Street he
volunteered to turn king's evidence. The eleven prisoners
seized these items as clues to their future, also fuel for their
fears; discussed them with each other and their guards,
brooded on them in the long days, dreamed of them in the
comfortless nights.

The snobbery of Newgate surprised any who hadn't been
there before. Far from being ill-treated, they were honoured by
other prisoners and even by the guards for the audacity of their
crime. Thistlewood was put in a cell for prisoners of rank or
wealth, without having to pay, and allowed a coal fire, extra
blankets and furniture. Meals were brought on a tray, to spare
him eating with common criminals. On Sunday evenings the
governor came to sit with him, ordering a bottle of claret and
glasses to be sent in, and they talked politics like any two
middle-aged gentlemen. The governor showed remarkable
liberalism for an official whose life had been confined to the
prison service; Thistlewood, who had read and travelled more,
discussed ideas and places that the governor had hardly heard
of; and each, from different views, compared the prisons they
knew. But though Lord Sidmouth's ruling on pen and paper
was ignored, the normal precautions for a dangerous prisoner
weren't relaxed; a guard was kept in Thistlewood's cell all day,
and two at night.

He sat on his chair, elbows on the table, knuckles screwed
into his cheeks, dark eyes fixed on the wall. He took snuff from
his silver box, held it in his fingertips for five minutes, ten
minutes, without seeming to know it was there, then remembered and put it to his nostrils; or forgot and dropped it on the
floor. He asked for books and newspapers, read and wrote,
abandoned them in disgust and asked for more. At night his

sleep was often broken by a sudden great cry, 'Ha! I've got you now!' or, 'The old grub!' ringing through the little stone room, and his bed became a vortex of agitation. After a struggle he would wake up, his eyes burning, not knowing where he was, but would laugh on seeing the guards and say, 'What strange things we dream about,' and lie sleepless till morning.

*

. . . I see Clothilde, the only woman I have stayed in love with – for nearly thirty years, through two marriages. She teases me as she always did. Provocative, peevish, a bitch . . . and I see Jane, my first wife. Older than Clothilde, older than myself, the daughter of a rich Lincoln squire who hated me. Nobody else would marry her even for the money. But he hadn't long to live, I could be patient. Jane was flat and cold like the Lincolnshire countryside. I knew how Clothilde would laugh if she saw my English wife. I never told Jane about Paris or the revolution or anything that mattered. I used to put my hand out for her body and find her bony bloodless corpse and wish for a roundness, a hillock of flesh under my fingers. When she was pregnant the bulge was a tight hard thing that got in the way, uncomfortable for us both. But I consoled myself with her wealth. It was the only time I have had money to spend and I squandered it, gambled it away. Sometimes I thought of it, instead of Clothilde, when I was in bed with Jane. It delighted me to abuse the dead squire's hoard. Some of it, out of spite and a hope that he might be watching, I gave to revolutionary societies. But in the end he tricked me. Jane and the baby died, her fortune went back to her family. I felt nothing at her death except the loss of my child and the sense of a chance wasted, of justice unavenged. I should have been more generous with her money, to finance the revolution. Instead, with creditors following the funeral, I pleaded a few days for my grief and fled to London. I never went back to Lincoln . . . I see Jane in her coffin with the baby, no more pale and cold than usual.

. . . I see Susan the first time at a meeting in a London hall. I was on the platform, she was in the front row. Her long gold hair and laughing eyes below me, almost crying at my speech. I was making it for her, I had never done it so well. We met outside and walked through Hyde Park in the evening. Lord Castlereagh was walking there too and smiled, envying us, I thought. I was proud to be with such a handsome woman, but Susan made a rude gesture with her fingers at him. I led her away before she could do worse. Sometimes she spoke at meetings, and I watched her standing in front of me on the platform, neat and smart and dignified – and mine. Such passion! Nothing bloodless about Susan. She had the appetite of a warrior, a virago – she ate me. People were surprised how she could shout. She quoted the *Rights of Man* by heart, she ran ahead and looked back and laughed and waited for me to catch up. But Susan was never really mine, she never let me catch her. Always ahead of me or somewhere else. When Julian was born she didn't stop, she took him to demonstrations and marches all over the country. We were the Thistlewoods on tour.

*

A wet morning at the end of April. Several hundred people waited at the side gate of the Old Bailey to see the black maria from Newgate. Only twenty were allowed in court after the defence lawyer had reserved most of the public seats, but the crowd had stood in the rain since early morning and wouldn't be disappointed. There wasn't much hope of seeing the eleven men: the van would be driven into the yard and the gates shut before they were let out. But having it pass so close was worth the wait, and the arrival of lawyers and jurymen and some of the wives was a consolation. To the disgust of many women in the crowd Mrs Davidson wasn't black; and Mrs Thistlewood had only to glare at the people, toss her gold hair and walk proudly past, for them to feel the rasp of her contempt and the thrill of their own shame.

One man felt a special thrill, of something more delicate than shame. At the back of the crowd in his huge brown overcoat with the collar turned up, Edwards tugged at his pale beard. He had promised Hobhouse not to try to get into court, but there was no harm in coming to stand here. Not much could be seen from inside a black maria and he was safe against the wall. It was a curious excitement: a need to witness the beginning of the end, a wish to attend a typical London occasion, to take away with him. Hobhouse had promised that by next week, for him as well as for the prisoners, there would be no more chances. Or perhaps one more: the possibility of another little job for

Edwards before emigrating.

The rain had drifted away leaving brightness in the sky and puddles in the street, when someone gave a shout. The people looked up, a soft gasp arose. The black maria had turned the corner and was approaching. No need to hurry, there wasn't far to go, they had plenty of time. Haste would be unseemly and the eleven men inside, least of all, could hardly be impatient.

The horses slipped, the springs of the van creaked under their load, a man shouted, 'Good luck, the lot of you!' and it was over – the police forming a line across the closed gates, the people left wondering in the empty street. In time they strolled away and the spring sun coaxed a wisp of vapour from the puddles.

Edwards had nothing to do. He couldn't go to the pubs or coffee shops where he was known. London had no use for him now, nor he for it. On top of the thousand pounds for delivering Thistlewood he could count on a fair bounty from the ministry and a passage to the colonies. It was part of the arrangement, though nothing was written down and the sum and destination had never been fixed. With luck he would get a plot of land somewhere, it wasn't unheard of, depending on the outcome of the trial. He favoured Canada. But there remained this little job next week. He could guess what it was. Till then his time was free for worry. He turned down towards Ludgate Hill, he might go and sit in St Paul's. He spent several hours a day there, feeling safe in a cathedral.

*

Eight wives sat at the front of the public gallery: Susan Thistlewood at the end, then Celia Ings who had come up from Portsmouth, Mary Brunt, Mary Tidd, Sarah Davidson, Caroline Harrison, Amelia Bradburn and Mary Strange. The three other prisoners – Cooper, Wilson, Gilchrist – had no wives or none who cared to see the trial. Men who might be fathers or brothers sat behind the women, with the twenty who had been let in from the street. They watched lawyers, clerks, reporters assembling; a man unpacking a case of weapons, ammunition, bombs; the jury filing into their box; the lion and unicorn above the throne, and Justice with sword and scales; the empty dock.

In a moment the dock was very full. Eleven prisoners, with twice as many policemen keeping them apart. All looked pale, startled, dazzled at coming up from the cells into the bright court. Hauled out of a hole into the daylight. A shaft of April sunshine slanted from a window, they blinked and screwed their eyes to see the court. It was smaller than they expected: only a few feet from them to their lawyers and wives, and hardly room in the dock for so many. They stared out and the public, jury, reporters stared back.

'Court rise!'

Everyone was suddenly upright for the judge to come out of the panelling and move to his throne below the lion and unicorn. A tough old bird settling into its nest. A rare species, almost extinct. Few to be found except in places like this, but reluctant to die out. A flurry of black and scarlet plumage, a hooked beak on a flabby grey face hanging under the ancient coils of a wig. It returned the lawyers' bow before dropping out of sight behind the desk, leaving only the wig above. Everyone sat down. Only the men in the dock were stranded on their feet for the rigmarole of calling over and swearing the jury. Prisoners at the bar: but they weren't handcuffed or chained, they could shift among the policemen to look around. After two months in Newgate there was a lot to see.

Then before anyone could stop him, or see how he got there or wonder what he was doing, a shabby old man stood on a chair behind the lawyers' table, lifted his hat carefully up to the dock and put it on the rail; pointed to Thistlewood, then to the hat. As if expecting it, Thistlewood picked five oranges out of the hat. The man reached up, took it down and shuffled from the court. But a policeman was sent after him and another was told to take the oranges from the prisoner: they might be bombs or poison, they must be examined. A discussion was held, a book was consulted, the wigged bird in his nest was seen to nod and the oranges were returned to the dock.

The clerk of the court, in a voice that came from all corners of the room, from everywhere except himself, began calling out names.

'Arthur Thistlewood, gentleman.' A policeman prodded him, he pushed the oranges into his pockets and stepped forward, two policemen close behind. 'Hold up your hand.' But he didn't look much of a figure in his old blue coat, one hand up, the other on the dock. He would like to be defiant, disdainful, fiery, if he couldn't be handsome. After prison anyone would feel pale and shrunk, even a Jacobin. Thistlewood was forty-nine last birthday.

'James Ings, butcher.' Little Ings bounced to the rail and held up his hand, then turned it into a wave to his wife. Good for Ings.

'John Thomas Brunt, shoemaker.' The names were false but he couldn't disclaim them. He looked puzzled and nervous between policemen with his hand up.

'Richard Tidd, shoemaker.' Tidd was the oldest apart from Thistlewood and the sorriest. He always knew he would end up here, he had told his wife so, and smiled at her unhappily.

'William Davidson, labourer.' The Jamaican had a small Bible in his hand with bits of paper between the pages. Thistlewood, who hadn't moved at the other names, shut his eyes in pain when Davidson was called. They had got the black man; probably Lord Sidmouth made a point of it.

The five men filled the front row of the dock. The other six stood behind and raised their hands when they were called.

'John Harrison, unemployed.'

'Charles Cooper, sailor.'

'William Bradburn, carpenter.'

'James Wilson, tailor.'

'John Strange, salesman.'

'James Gilchrist, shoemaker.'

The clerk began reading out the charge.

*

. . . I see the gift of oranges I took to Robespierre – his favourite fruit. And this queer old tramp passing up his hat with oranges in it. I wonder who he is and how he knew. Not a word spoken, just five oranges. That is the finest thing, to be loved by strangers who aren't afraid. Jesus had it when he needed it. The court is full of friends. The sympathy in a policeman's eye, the compassion of a clerk, the voice outside the black maria, wishing us luck. And those twelve men of the jury – they will understand and feel and know. Like the first night in Fox Court with twelve apostles, twelve good men and true. I haven't felt it in a court before, it has always been hostility or ridicule. This time I'm not frightened.

. . . I see myself standing at the front, the place of honour. Arthur Thistlewood, gentleman – the only one among eleven of us. Eleven, out of thirty in the stable that night, is the best Lord Sidmouth can do. But he's pleased with himself, the old grub, rubbing his hands somewhere. On his cock, trying for a stand. Small hope. In church probably – in St Paul's, not far away. Or he's here in the Old Bailey, under a wig or dressed as a policeman. Perhaps it isn't a real judge up there, but Sidmouth . . . I see him in the Speaker's chair thirty years ago and the look he gave, the tiny private sneer.

. . . I see Susan among the women, her pride and confidence, her gold hair more lustrous than the coat of arms above the judge. But today she is a stranger too. The distance between us is the world. She doesn't love me as a man, but worships the revolutionary. She's at my feet, kissing them like a pilgrim at the statue of her saint. She deceives me, I deceive myself, we enjoy it. There's our work to do, our revolution. We are allies, not lovers . . . I see the gallery in the Paris parliament full of laughing shouting women, but these English ones only stare at us, then look away and listen.

. . . I see the clerk reading out the charge. The hard legal voice rattles round the court, but the words aren't hard, they're soft and pulpy, they have no stone inside. It's like being pelted with tomatoes . . . *'being subjects of our sovereign lord not having the fear of God in their hearts but being seduced by the devil and withdrawing the love obedience and fidelity which every true subject should bear . . .'* Withdrawing the love is what Susan did. Or she never had it. She loves Julian perhaps, our son . . . *'with force and arms in the parish of St Marylebone maliciously and traitorously among themselves and with other false traitors whose names are unknown . . .'* But they aren't unknown, Lord Sidmouth has them in his office, supplied by Edwards. And what is a false traitor? . . . *'did compass imagine and intend to deprive and depose our sovereign . . .'*

I'm not sure when I first knew who Edwards was. Knowledge stretches back from consciousness into the dark. Perhaps it was the moment I saw the door opening in the shuttered room. It came to me at a stroke, quicker than the pistol poking round the door. Edwards had brought me to that house, he alone knew where I was. Or a minute earlier – the jingle of keys outside the door. I must have known then, in my half sleep . . . *'in order to fulfil perfect and bring to effect their most evil and wicked treason . . .'* Perhaps I always knew it was Edwards, and defied it . . . *'did assemble meet conspire consult and agree to assassinate kill and murder the*

95

members of the cabinet employed by our sovereign . . .'

I knew, but did nothing. I knew when I met him running from the stable and he said he could take me to a place to hide in. When he went down the ladder to fetch beer and gin before the police arrived. When he suggested the stable for our meetings. He had been offered it for a studio, I can guess who by. He had the answers, the friends – half the men were brought by Edwards. He was the one with any money, who could pay a man's rent and buy a newspaper. Once he was walking the streets with his little statues, in broken shoes and no socks, then suddenly he was well dressed and had time to spare. I knew it then. Perhaps even before I met him, when I heard about a young man who wanted to get in touch with me. I heard from a prison guard, I should have been suspicious . . . I see the eagerness on a young man's face, the future in his eyes. It goes so fast, it's finished before anything has happened. Forty-nine last birthday.

. . . I see a child's birthday long ago in Lincolnshire. Meat pies down the table, jugs of beer, bowls of cream. And the child – a long-faced boy, impetuous and insolent, treated by grown-ups as a force, a power of his own. They watched him, careful not to let him frighten them, and wondered what he would grow into. I wondered too. I read books, went out on the road, talked to travellers about the world, walked eighteen miles to Lincoln to listen to a speech . . . *'did conspire to set fire to and destroy houses and barracks used for the soldiers troops and forces of our sovereign lord and to provide combustibles . . .'*

On the way home from Lincoln in the dark I broke through a hedge and set fire to a hayrick. Walking on, I stopped often to watch it burn and could still see it from my bedroom, an orange furnace on the flat land. It was my father's hayrick . . . I see the farmers shouting next day, my father the loudest. Harvests had been bad for years, the rick burners were hated. If they were caught they were hanged at Lincoln . . . I see a dish of rotten boiled potatoes, our usual meal, with butter and a mug of tea. The potatoes were always rotten . . . *'did compose and prepare addresses and proclamations containing solicitations and incitements to the subjects of our sovereign lord presenting that their tyrants were destroyed . . .'*

It must be the longest charge he has ever read, composed and prepared by his sovereign Lord Sidmouth. I feel tired, thirsty, standing in this hot room close to the others. Policemen pressing round, breathing behind my ears. I shall faint if we have to stand much longer – the oldest in the dock . . . '*armed and arrayed in a warlike manner that is to say with guns muskets blunderbusses pistols swords bayonets and pikes and with quantities of ammunition that is to say gunpowder bullets slugs and grenades being then and there unlawfully maliciously and traitorously assembled and gathered against our sovereign lord most wickedly did ordain levy and make public war against our sovereign lord within his realm and did attempt and endeavour by force and arms to subvert and destroy the constitution and government as by law established and to deprive and depose our sovereign lord of and from the style honour and name of the imperial crown to the evil example of all others . . .*'

. . . I see him putting aside his paper and picking up another. His voice doesn't falter, merely switches from the charge to something else. The words stream from his mouth without a break, filling the crowded court till the place is bursting, there's no room for more. Then they stop, the mouth is closed, the voice shut off. The last words missed me, but I know they were meant for me. I look round the court, searching for them. Nobody will help. I find them lying at the edge of memory, addressed to the prisoner Thistlewood.

'How say you, Arthur Thistlewood – are you guilty or not guilty of the treason you stand charged with?'

'Not guilty.' My own words now lie on top of all the others.

'How will you be tried?'

'By God and my country.'

The clerk addresses the prisoner Ings. In a loud voice the butcher says he will be tried by the laws of reason. The judge flutters behind his desk, a policeman whispers – the prisoner must plead in the proper way. Well, he will accept the laws of God and England, but the laws of God being those of reason he will be acquitted because he can prove his innocence.

The rest plead not guilty and will be tried by God and England. Having spoken we have staked our presence, our life. Our voices have been heard, we exist. It makes us bold, and we ask to be given chairs. More fluttering from the judge and a consultation, then the distant voice of the clerk. The trial is likely to last several days, therefore the court will let the prisoners sit. Chairs and benches are handed up into the dock and we thank the court. There will be journeys back to

Newgate, nights in prison, morning reappearances. I take the five oranges from my pocket and pass four to the others in front – Ings, Brunt, Tidd, Davidson. We peel them, giving the skin to the policemen.

. . . I see the lawyer for the prosecution standing up, bowing to the judge, grasping the lapels of his gown with both hands. And the lawyer for the defence, standing, bowing, grasping. They are interchangeable or the same man, one man between the two. Obsequious, patronising, confident – they know the secrets, they will share them with the jury. They speak about themselves, their difficulties, their precious duty. They speak for the rest of the week, the rest of their lives, up and down, one after the other – I forget which is which and it doesn't matter. They never look at the dock. Not a glance at the men they're accusing or defending, saving or destroying. They air their arrogance and condescension . . . I see the back of their gowns and wigs and sometimes the corner of a face, but never their eyes. Perhaps one is Sidmouth. Perhaps both are.

*

'Gentlemen, you have been called to one of the most solemn tasks that can fall on Englishmen. The charge of treason has peculiar consequences not only for the prisoners in the dock. The whole country was touched by the evil of this conspiracy and will be touched by the outcome of this trial. Your verdict will affect the lives of those eleven men, but I will show you that for England too . . . '

'These men have a right to call upon me to do my duty fearlessly, but I have another duty to my country. I mustn't try by any talents I possess – if I do possess such talents – to pervert the law. With these duties weighing me almost to the earth I pray that I may rely upon that Power which we all look up to . . . '

'You must guard against any suggestion, any whispered insinuation stealing into your breasts and minds, that these are the men about whom so much has been said and that it could never have been said without their being guilty . . . '

'It is five centuries since that statute was passed which Englishmen regard as the protection of their dearest rights . . . '

'I may not prove to your satisfaction every one of the acts, but I shall prove sufficient . . . '

'Feeling every pity, as you ought to feel, for the prisoners and their unhappy wives and children – forty children, I believe . . .'

'Awful as it may seem it was decided – yes, by Englishmen it was decided – to assassinate the king's ministers. Nobody can doubt that in the wild vision of these men the assassination was to be followed by an English revolution. My learned friend will claim that the plan was so absurd that it could never have been seriously laid, but as you and I know – as anyone of experience and common sense knows – men with heated passions . . .'

'It has been said that in a secret conspiracy there are things known only to the conspirators and God . . .'

'Luckily one of them had serious visitings of compunction and felt it his duty to reveal the plot. You might think that he should have refused at the beginning, but men's minds are formed differently – such is the bounty of God – and while some can see things in a moment, others take longer. The witness Adams is one of those . . .'

'Among men devoted to evil purposes there are sometimes to be found those who are ingenious in devising further evil and who become informers. You might expect some principle of honour by which even criminals are faithful to each other, but Adams is destitute . . .'

'My learned friend will tell you that the charge can only be proved by an accomplice and that such a man isn't to be believed unless he is supported by more creditable witnesses. But if his evidence isn't admitted there will be the offer of impunity to tempt all future conspirators. It is not the law of England to reject the evidence of a man against his friends. You will hear him with caution and watch him carefully, but if he is confirmed in one detail then you are to believe the rest . . .'

'When an evil and wicked witness tells you a tale that is not only improbable but absurd, will you not dismiss him? Can you – dare you – take the lives of eleven men on evidence that wouldn't justify the accuracy of a laundry bill? . . .'

Adams' face hung in front of the eleven men, twisted further by the self-mockery of a free pardon. Dodging and slithering, he got out the story he had learnt and gave away things he may have wished to hide. Was it true that he had once boasted in a pub that he knew a simple way of making money, and produced seventy pounds to prove it? Had he taken a man to Hyde Park

99

and shown him how to accost a likely gentleman and accuse him of an unnatural offence – too vile to be named in court – and then demand ten pounds for his silence? Did he or did he not claim to have lain in wait outside the house of a certain cabinet minister – also to be nameless – and caught the minister by the collar and offered to tell the newspapers about his visits to a brothel? Had he or had he not arranged with like-minded friends for a prostitute to accompany that minister to a house where she undressed and revealed, to the minister's astonishment, that she wasn't a woman? Had he at that moment, with his friends, burst into the room and accused the minister of a sin from which the minds of everyone here must shrink? Had he exploited the minister's confusion to relieve him of his money? Had he repeatedly reminded the minister of the incident and threatened, to his own profit, to expose facts which would ruin the minister's career and estrange him from his wife?

Impaled by questions Adams wriggled in agony, then was led between two policemen to the dock. He stared at each prisoner with his single eye, the other sunk in its socket and switched permanently to one side – half a face for half a man. His twisted jaw quivered a yard from his friends, he couldn't hide his fright and shame – accusing with his Cyclops eye, appealing to them. It was too easy to despise him: nobody knew what he had been through in Bow Street. Thistlewood kept his contempt for the kind of justice that could allow it; stared firmly back and offered his silver snuff-box. Adams flinched, then shuffled along to identify them one by one. Though Brunt hurled himself at Adams' throat and had to be held down, the others caught Thistlewood's composure. It wasn't Adams who should be throttled: behind the sneak who saw a chance to save his neck was a far worse man.

'Gentlemen, you have heard from the witness Adams how his conscience was alarmed and he vowed that if he could be spared he would reveal everything. You have heard him swear that he has given us the truth because God told him so, but I ask you if the truth isn't that Adams would send those eleven to the scaffold sooner than be hanged . . . '

'You have heard him describe how a nation was to be plunged into revolution, an empire overturned . . . '

'He who failed to murder his allotted victim was himself to be murdered. But how was he to be tried? Was he to be massacred without benefit of judge or jury? And who was the last assassin, to murder the rest if they all failed? These are secrets which the imagination of Adams – the source of contaminated falsehood which you're asked to swallow – doesn't supply. See how this wretched tale crumbles into dust when touched by the text of truth. This is the delirium of dark delusion, the fiction of a disordered fantasy, more ridiculous than all the dramas of the stage or the romance of novels . . . '

'I must remind you, gentlemen, that Adams served his country in a famous regiment, the Blues . . . '

'You have listened to a description of the people's government, you have been privileged to attend a session of the members – these same hungry, miserable, obscure men in the dock today – you have watched the prisoner Tidd in the presidential chair, with all the dignity of office . . . '

'My learned friend doesn't believe this sack is big enough for two human heads, despite the promise of the prisoner Ings, but I assure you . . . '

'We come to the business of their exchequer and the prisoner Brunt begins as usual with an oath, holy fucking Christ – you won't suppose that I repeat it with any pleasure – holy fucking Christ, he still has a one pound note and he'll give it for a treat, but gentlemen, one pound wouldn't buy a cup of tea for them all, yet it was their total treasury . . . '

'Let us rejoice that London is free from the atrocities that befell Paris . . . '

'We've done pretty well so far. We've got possession of London, we've blocked the bridges, we've sealed the ports, we've surrounded the king's palace and the soldiers, poor souls, are too lazy to rescue him. Some of us are sitting in the Mansion House while others are wandering about with sacks of fireballs, setting alight to buildings for our amusement. But good God, gentlemen, are these dreams? Eleven men would be lost inside the Mansion House . . . '

The eleven were lost among the policemen, day after day, all week. Sometimes one raised a hand to the gallery, passed a message to a lawyer, smiled at something he heard or remembered or imagined. They often yawned. The court was full of warm stale breath, the deadly stuff of law. Little Ings shook with anger and began to splutter, but was stopped by a wave from his wife. Davidson took out his Bible, removed the bits of paper and put them back in other places. Tidd blushed several times a day. Each morning the strange old man came with his hat full of oranges.

Thistlewood watched the jury. They never made a note, perhaps they couldn't write, but sat without moving, twelve dull beings asleep with their eyes open, with a dubious task ahead: not a glint or flicker to show that any thought had reached a human mind. When a grenade was handed to them they passed it round like a turnip. Thistlewood took snuff and the lawyers talked.

'Gentlemen, this case is vital to the young people of today, to your children and future generations . . .'

'Gentlemen, it isn't the value of these men's lives that is the question, but the danger of a precedent . . .'

'When I was a young man every drop of my blood thrilled with horror as I read of the atrocities which polluted Paris. All the diabolical machinery that dark and savage minds could invent was put into operation, metaphysical murderers and speculative republicans wrought scenes from which my soul still recoils, human heads were paraded through the public streets, virtue was violated, innocence sacrificed, nobility destroyed, the sacred institutions of wisdom were torn down and the worst barbarities inflicted on the royal family, while butchery became a pastime . . .'

'You have everything here to raise the passions and garnish my friend's case. But where was this great conspiracy concocted? Why, in a little second floor back room. Where was the battle fought? In a stable. Where did the traitors meet? In a hayloft. How were they armed? With that powerful display of rusty weapons on the table . . .'

'Let me pray that God may direct your minds and souls . . .'

'Let your verdict be delivered in justice and tempered in mercy . . .'

'I must warn you of the danger from your own emotions . . .'

'Whether you decide that their lives should be narrowed to the limits of one more week or continue for as long as Providence may please . . .'

'Gentlemen, the eyes of England are on you . . .'

On Thursday afternoon the lawyers sat down and there was silence for several minutes before the judge, with a rustling of his costume, began his summing up. He spoke rapidly in a low monotone that could hardly be heard, but nobody doubted he was on the side of severity. He was ignorant of reality, estranged from life, inhabiting a world of secret formulas. His mind was closed, riveted to the past, bound and collecting dust like a library. He posed as an expert, his opinion was paramount, though he knew nothing about the nature of the men he judged.

'Gentlemen of the jury,' he was heard to say, 'you have listened to the eloquence of two distinguished lawyers . . . ' Somebody hissed in the gallery, nobody moved. The judge went on for hours. Occasionally, with a mouthful of air washed down with a sip of water, a few sentences were saved from the impenetrable drone. 'No motive can begin to excuse this crime, but it would be wrong to let indignation colour your judgment. You stand as the guardians of safety between the prosecution and the possibility of an injustice.'

A man opened a window for a shaft of freedom from outside. In the street, out in the April sunshine, a slogan was being chanted: '*Power to the people, power to the people* . . . ' The man shut the window.

'The prisoners claim that they're being tried for their opinions. I direct you to have none of that. In this country it is not an offence to have opinions in opposition to the government. We don't have political trials.'

A girl stood up in the gallery and began arguing with the judge, but was hustled out before he noticed. For a moment, with the door open, the chanting could be heard again: '*Power to the people* . . . '

'You mustn't hold it against a man that he isn't a normal member of society. He is normal in his own eyes.'

Ings shouted, 'Disgusting,' and was stifled.

Thursday afternoon passed. Beams of spring sunlight flattened through the windows and faded, and the court adjourned till tomorrow. On Friday morning the beams slanted from the other side, but nobody was chanting in the street. The judge picked up his voice where he had left it.

'It was an abomination in the view of every decent person.' He went on for two more hours. 'There has been talk of the sentence which might follow your verdict. You must be sensible about this. You have to steel your hearts to see that justice is done for everyone in England.' Imperceptibly the court began to stir. Tiny movements showed the recapture of interest, the quickening of anticipation. 'Obeying in the name of God the dictates of your conscience . . . ' The policemen sat up higher and straightened their tunics. The long week was nearly over. 'If you feel satisfied that a conspiracy to levy war against his majesty has been made out, you will have the painful duty of pronouncing the prisoners guilty. But if anything has raised in your minds a doubt that this was ever contemplated, you will give it in favour of the prisoners and have the more pleasant duty of pronouncing them not guilty. I know that your verdict will do justice to your country and yourselves . . . '

The throne, dock, jury box were emptied. Two hours later a note came from the jury asking for a copy of the treason statute, five hundred years old. Another two hours later they returned. They would do their duty with a bungling, half-hearted shiftiness. Twelve clumsy pairs of eyes rolled around the court, resting on the coat of arms, the table of exhibits, the floor, everywhere but on the dock. Guilty or not guilty – how could they tell? What was the difference? Was it important? Were they doing it properly? Had they got it right? They seemed to appeal to the judge, asking his approval. He would know the answer, he was a professional, they were just simple fellows from outside. It wasn't fair. How could they choose between life and death when they had no knowledge of either? They knew nothing, except that the job was finished and they could go home. They were the guilty ones.

The prisoners stood.

'Gentlemen of the jury, are you agreed in your verdict?'

The answer came from nobody. From nowhere. From the woodwork, the street, the suburbs, the towns and villages and countryside of England, the estuaries and coasts, from the sea infinitely nudging the shore and rolling to the world's end, to roll back into the Old Bailey one sunny, deadly Friday afternoon.

'How say you – are the prisoners at the bar guilty of the treason they are charged with, or not guilty?'

It came in one word from a stranger in the crowd. From the hole in a man's face with teeth and tongue, in a thin metallic voice that shocked the silence and scratched the taut transparent air and fixed itself instantly and for ever on the walls. No blur, no inflection, no echo – just two syllables, one word of death. People looked round to see where it had gone. Gone like a ball that fell out of an empty box, a mouse that found its hole. The trick was done. Before the word began the eleven men in the dock breathed, palpitated, existed like other men. When it ended they were phantoms. The panelled room was a coffin, the sunlight and pure sky through the windows were the lining of a grave. One word to end a week of words: to end eleven men. After it the silence came back into the court.

The silence lasted a minute, an hour, a life.

*

. . . I see Robespierre at the Festival of the Supreme Being, alone with his soul. He wore his sky blue coat, white silk waistcoat embroidered with silver, yellow silk trousers, shoes with gold buckles. People whispered of his immodesty, and laughed because he stood apart and had two bouquets of flowers when everybody else had one. People say anything about their enemies: they said he was a coward. But it was he who set the statue of Atheism alight and raised the revolution above mob politics. He was the priest and prophet who saw beyond the streets.

I watched him during the last weeks – my own last weeks in Paris too. Didn't he remind me, Clothilde asked, of another man who emerged from obscurity at the age of thirty for a brief career of teaching and conversion? Hadn't I noticed that Arras was in the north of France, as Nazareth was in the north of Palestine? Wasn't it odd that Robespierre retired from public life for forty days before returning to Paris for a final testament? There was a plan about his life, a pattern of coincidences that suggested they were ordained or chosen but not fortuitous. He was fulfilling a mission, he came to Paris at a moment of need, he lived out his destiny. He was a democrat who rebelled against the tyrants, who led men to liberty and equality, who was irresistible and uncompromising, whose home was simple, whose life was celibate – the same was precisely true of Jesus. Clothilde told me, half in mischief, half in awe, that children were brought to him to be blessed.

. . . I see him that summer day at the Festival of the Supreme Being in his best suit – transfigured, Clothilde said. She believed that he wanted to be assassinated, he had arranged it on purpose. The pack was on his heels, there was a Judas at

hand, he would make a perfect target. The cult, the conspicu-
ousness, the effrontery were deliberate. It would be a good
occasion, a sacrifice at the point of triumph. He had a sense of
timing, he knew he must die soon and this would be the
moment . . . I see him trembling in his gaudy clothes, the
nervous twitching of his cheeks, the convulsions that shook his
shoulders, the tremor of his eyelids. It wasn't fear: he hoped
that death would come, any minute. The lamb that lay down on
the altar, ready for the knife – but it didn't happen that day, he
had to wait.

It wasn't a reprieve, for like Jesus he had his death
postponed. The agony had begun: all that remained was the
passion. He knew it wouldn't be long, but it would be on the
scaffold, not in the temple. He accepted it rapturously,
awaiting the glory that was to come. Yet people called him
cowardly. In his last speech, with the league of villains so
powerful he couldn't escape, he promised to surrender without
regret and leave a memory of himself which we would
vindicate. The similarity wasn't lost. After his arrest, when he
was in prison, we heard a clap of thunder over Paris. Clothilde
was serious when she said he had called for it himself.

. . . I see him on the way to the guillotine, the *via dolorosa*. We
stood in the street to watch the carts. He shared one with two
friends – two robbers probably, Clothilde said. His jaw had
been shot off, a bandage was tied round his head – a crown of
thorns. A woman shouted, 'Your majesty seems to be in pain.'
He wore his sky blue coat. The procession kept stopping, held
up by the crowd – the stations of the cross. Everyone joined in
the cruelty, the sarcasm, the hounding. It was all familiar:
another woman ran out to Robespierre with a sponge soaked in
sour wine. It's true: I was there, and envied him.

Clothilde dragged me with the crowd to the Place de la
Révolution . . . I see his face when the bandage was pulled off,
the moment before the blade fell. So much for apotheosis. His
head lay on the block and I saw that it knew and understood,
and so did I. It was waiting to the last fraction of a second and I
waited with it, listening for the last noise. It heard the clang of
steel coming down, it *must* have heard it. The noise was in its
ears when the head was severed. What was in them when it fell
into the basket?

. . . I see the judge coaxing the verdict from the jury.

Sometimes I believe it really is Lord Sidmouth up there. He has put on a wig and gown and slipped in for the occasion. There can't be two like that . . . I see the jury, the twelve men who condemned us, and Adams between two policemen staring ahead with his lopsided eye. The obscenity of that man, dragged to court to betray his friends – but I have no feelings for him: he doesn't exist, he is less than nobody.

. . . I still see Edwards, but not distinctly. His face has faded these last weeks, disintegrated in my memory as if eaten by disease. Poor man, to live with that. He can't last long. I forgive him from the bottom of my heart. I would choose a traitor's death rather than a hundred years to live with a million pounds to spend, if it was the life that Edwards has left to him.

*

'You stand convicted of treason. What have you to say why the court shouldn't give you judgment to die according to the law?'

Thistlewood stepped forward and spoke slowly in little jerks: 'What have I to say? This is a mockery – that's what I have to say. You went through the ceremony without the justice. Your vengeance will be gratified with the blood of a man you call a traitor. All I say is, there's more patriotism in my heart than in any of the tyrants who rule the people's lives. I've no hope of justice from you. Any justice you ever had has been swallowed by greed. And I don't want pity instead. I despise your pity. Soon I shall be dead. I shall be glad. The same peaceful night, when I'm sleeping in my grave, will bring you nightmares. I don't care for my life – that surprises you, I expect. All I want is to rescue my name while I can. I'm proud that the way I took to kill the cabinet was more honourable than the way the cabinet took to kill me. I always admired the assassination of tyrants. If they put themselves above the law they can't be brought to justice. Except by the hand of one man. The people are starving, in case you didn't know. When they dared protest they were trampled on and killed, women and babies – you know as well as I. And the king thanked the murderers. If a spark of liberty existed the people would have risen, but they didn't. So somebody had to act. My feelings were too intense to bear – you wouldn't understand that. The lives of the murderers had to be the requiem for the people they murdered – if you believe that kind of thing. That's when I met Edwards.

He isn't a man at all. I don't know what he is. There isn't a word for him. He's a disease without a name. I'm sorry for him, if you want to know. And sorry for the people who employ him. You ask, what have I to say? Rebellion is a public duty now. You talk of the sovereign king. Only the people are sovereign, but there's nothing they can do. Or nothing they want to do. They surrender. That's my disappointment. I don't despise them. England is in chains. I shall leave it without regret. I'm only sad that it's a country of tyrants and slaves. And cowards. But the time will come. Not long. I shall be under ground. What have I to say? One day I shall be remembered.'

Ings spoke in a rush: 'I left school and never learnt to make a speech so I'm no good, except I got into this through Edwards when I couldn't find work, but probably you don't know what it is to have nothing to keep your wife and children, and I hope they'll live to see justice to their bleeding country if they don't starve first, but if you want my opinion starvation's worse than assassination and like Mr Thistlewood said, I don't mind dying if you'll send Edwards to die with me, because they found me with a sword, that's all, and there's nothing against having a meeting, it's the law of England which King John signed in the open air by the river, which probably you know about, till Lord Sidmouth wiped out something we had fought for, hundreds of years ago, and anyone can do that, it isn't clever if you've got the power and Lord Sidmouth knew all about this for months, long before I got into it.' Little Ings faltered and a sob struck the waiting court. His mouth curled and quivered, he sniffed, rubbed his sleeve across his face and blinked: 'I'm like a bullock that's driven into Smithfield to be sold,' and broke down, speaking through a gush of tears: 'My life's no use unless I get a living for my family, but I can't tell you my feelings about that, probably you can guess, and I can't speak well so I'll stop and thank you for your patience, but I never went drinking or anything like that or to the radical meetings, and that man Adams – you saw him, he'd hang his father, he'd hang his God. There isn't any more, that's all I've got.'

Brunt stood up in a hurry, the biggest and loudest of them: 'I asked for a pen and paper to write this down but it wasn't allowed. What I have to say is very short. Looking round me, it makes my blood boil in my veins. The sacred name of justice has been prostituted for vile purposes. Those buggers' death was for the public good. That's why I joined. And I'm not the man to have ever stopped. I'm not a bloody shuttlecock – that bastard Edwards saw that. He saw I could be trusted to stick my neck out, even for the rope, sooner than go back on what I'd said. If I swore to kill the buggers I'd do it. Holy Christ, I'd have gone through it to the end or else be killed – it would have been an honour to die in Grosvenor Square that night.' His voice thickened, his face turned red. 'Looking round, what do I see? Men in power who discuss in parliament how they can starve the people. They've caused the death of millions. I don't care a farthing fuck for my life it it's to be sacrificed for liberty. I'll die with pleasure for the good of my country. As long as there's a nerve left in my body I'll fight the people's enemies. Torture me how you like, put me on the rack, cut me in quarters, you'll never break my spirit, you'll see. Make my wife a widow and my daughter an orphan – I'll go up there on the platform as cheerfully as I'm speaking now.'

Ings began shouting to show he wasn't weeping, and was suppressed by a policeman.

Tidd stood forward, the meekest, stammering and blushing: 'I only met Brunt because we had Christmas together and he asked a friend who could bring some gin. That was Edwards. Before that I never did anything with politics. I was a hard working man, sixteen or eighteen hours a day – I never had time off except on Sunday. They said there was a meeting and I knew it wasn't allowed because of Lord Sidmouth's law, but Edwards said this was for the reform in parliament and he had the word of authority, that's why I agreed to take the chair when they proposed it. Now I see why he said he had the word, because it was from the top, which you've seen yourselves. That's all I have to say and I've told the truth.'

Davidson opened his Bible. He was a Sunday school teacher, not just a black man pleading for his life: 'I haven't much to say except some verses from the sacred book. *He was oppressed and afflicted yet he opened not his mouth.* I was a harmless man all my life. I only got the blunderbuss because Edwards gave it to me. Man, I tell you – that's the truth and I lay my hand on my heart in the presence of God.' He turned up another page: '*If any mischief follow, then thou shalt give life for life.* I only went down Cato Street by chance. Edwards gave me the sword too. As for Adams – who is he but a poor working man who comes here for his day's pay and a meal, to swear away my life? *A false witness that uttereth lies is an abomination unto the Lord.* I have no friends but many children, and I ask you – are they to live in the knowledge that their father died a traitor's death? *A true witness delivereth souls, but a deceitful witness speaketh lies.* Has anyone identified me except Adams, who sold himself to the police? I'm a black man and my colour's against me, but my heart is as fair as any white man's. *Behold, if the witness hath testified falsely against his brother, then shall ye do unto him as he thought to do unto his brother.* Do I look like a plotter or assassin or traitor? If I do, then pronounce your sentence. I don't care what happens to me. I swear on my soul, which will soon appear before its Maker, that it's the truth. *A false witness shall not go unpunished, and he that speaketh lies shall perish.* I only feel for my children, and when I think of them I have no words. I'm unmanned. I am a child myself. I can't say more.'

A rustle of impatience passed through the court. The five men at the front of the dock had spoken, the six at the back were told to be brief. First Harrison: 'The evidence is lies, like what they said after St Peter's Fields. We haven't had a fair trial, we've been betrayed by villains.' Next Cooper: 'I have a lot to say but my friends think it's better not to say it.' Then Bradburn: 'I want to tell you that I was dragged into this by Edwards.' And Wilson: 'The same for me – I'm not gifted with the power of talk, but I wouldn't be here except for Edwards.' And Strange: 'That's right – betrayed by a villain you didn't dare bring into court.' Lastly Gilchrist: 'I never knew what was going on. I borrowed a penny from Edwards, that's all. I appeal to God who hears me and knows the truth.' He looked to the ceiling. 'I had no work and no money and no food, so I went to Cato Street where I was told there was something to eat.' He began to cry. 'They were cutting bread and cheese with a sword and I hadn't had anything all day. I asked what all the weapons were for and when they told me I tried to get away, but the police and soldiers came – oh God, I have nothing more.' He gave way to sobbing.

Thistlewood stepped forward once more: 'Sooner or later we shall be freed. You will hear from us again.'

'Silence!' came from the clerk.

The judge was seen to drink deeply from a glass of water. 'I am sorry, Thistlewood,' he said, 'to see an educated man in your present place. It was a warped idea that brought you here. You are revealed as a sinister man and a threat to the society you live in. One of the most precious rights of an Englishman is that he can express his opinions freely and protest against the government if he disagrees with it, but the day he tries to enforce his belief with violence he destroys that precious right. I don't say this to increase your guilt or aggravate your suffering, but to warn anyone who might hear of your example and benefit by your fate.' He drank more water and continued more ponderously. 'Any sensible person must regret that a man who has shown himself born for better things and who in early life must have received ideas of virtue from his parents and teachers, should have committed such a crime. Like other mortals who can only judge from the evidence I'm satisfied of your guilt. Your claims of innocence are only flattery to your soul and I beg you not to persist, lest the all-seeing Eye which reads all hearts should find that you have entered His presence with a lie in your mouth and perjury in your hand.' The other prisoners didn't deserve such consideration: 'You surrendered to the treacherous and irreligious influence of the newspapers, which seduced you from all morality and obligation to God and society. After a full and fair trial by a jury of your countrymen you have been found guilty. It is a proper verdict.'

Thistlewood opened his snuff-box.

'The sentence must be substantial. The public is entitled to protection. Everyone should know that men who behave like you must expect severe punishment.' In an extra flurry behind his desk the judge knocked over his water. To the tinkle of broken glass a velvet cap appeared in a pair of claws and was put on top of the wig – a small black crest on an old bird's head. The voice came from somewhere below it: 'If any of you should ultimately be spared, I trust you will bear in mind that you owe your lives to the mercy of your sovereign king and those men you conspired to murder.'

The prisoners looked round. They were in a theatre, on the stage. The king might appear in the audience at any moment, or anyway his ministers.

'It remains for me to pass the sentence of the law. But first I implore you to use the time left to you in praying for mercy from that almighty Power before whom you will shortly stand. Repent! – for through the merits of your Redeemer God's mercy is given to any man who truly and humbly repents.' He was a priest giving the blessing before sending the congregation home. 'The sentence of the law is that each of you be taken from here to the prison you came from, and from there you will be drawn on a hurdle to a place of execution and hanged by the neck until you are dead, and afterwards your heads will be cut from your bodies and your bodies divided into quarters, to be disposed of as his majesty thinks fit, and may God have mercy on your souls!'

'Amen!' the clerk said loudly and others repeated it. In the gallery a woman screamed and unbelievably a baby cried. The prisoners smiled, blinked, blushed, look at each other, took more snuff. Not one gasped or cried or swooned. In a moment they were chivvied from the dock and out of public sight. A box of chains was waiting. Eleven pairs of wrists and ankles were quickly shackled.

At the side gate the crowd was rewarded at last, this Friday afternoon, with a glimpse into the yard. The first man to be brought out, hooded with a blanket and led by two policemen, was recognised at once and hissed and booed: Adams would have been lynched if he hadn't been bustled into a cab. Then the eleven traitors were loaded into the black maria.

'Which is Thistlewood?'

'That's him!'

'When will it be?'

'They won't give them long.'

'Long live the hangman!'

'Good luck, gentlemen!'

The people pressed forward, milling round the van as it drove into the street and turned towards Newgate. Hands thumped on it and voices reached the men inside: abuse, encouragement, prayers – they couldn't hear anything distinctly.

*

On Saturday afternoon Sidmouth sat down and rang the silver bell. There was hardly anyone in the building – a clerk or two on weekend duty, a messenger, the coachman – but Hobhouse was waiting.

'Well Hobhouse, the privy council meeting . . . ' Sidmouth wouldn't go straight to the point, but made the most of

Hobhouse's impatience. And Hobhouse wouldn't show curiosity: the usual knotting of his fingers and slow writhing of his limbs.

'I made my report of the trial,' the minister said. 'There was great interest. The responsibility in our hands – you will understand. I've never known an atmosphere so grave and solemn, and his majesty felt it acutely. When I had finished there was a fitting silence. I had simply quoted the sentence of the court without elaboration, but I believe the council could hear the words as I could myself, from the judge's lips. They turned them over in their minds and examined the justice as well as the horror of those syllables. It was very moving. At last his majesty spoke. The pronouncement of his loyal judge, the report of his humble minister – now our gracious sovereign, a mortal being yet an imperial lord . . . ' Sidmouth's voice faltered, he blinked several times towards the king's portrait, then cleared his throat: 'We discussed the lives of eleven worthless men for more than an hour of a Saturday afternoon, when most people are at home and far from the cares of duty. Such is the extraordinary humanity of the English system. I've always said – and I said it today – that no good can come of tampering with the law of England. The law of gravity is an example of the same principle – they are laws of nature. There was no doubt in our minds that the verdict must be upheld, but we were anxious for every possibility of mercy to be explored. There must be sufferers – we were agreed on that, for the death penalty is an ordinance of God – but should all eleven pay the final price? We are not vindictive men, Hobhouse. Stern and just and patriotic, but not pitiless.'

Sidmouth stood up and walked to the window, leaving the secretary to his contortions. Eventually he came back: 'Among some of the council there existed a marked pity for the man Gilchrist. They argued that he was misled by the others who exploited his weak-mindedness and destitution. I couldn't share those feelings but I deferred.' Sidmouth paused. 'I needn't remind you, in cases of this kind it's often of benefit to the offender to be kept in ignorance of his fate. There's a temptation for a man who is given any hint of reprieve to rejoice too soon, before any real penal results have been observed. He may congratulate himself on his escape as if it was the consequence of his own exertions, not of a merciful authority.

These are the effects of leniency and are far from our intention.'
He paused again. 'Gilchrist will remain in prison during his
majesty's pleasure. There's no suggestion of his punishment
being remitted, but enquiries will be made into his character
and if they're satisfactory the man may one day receive the
royal pardon.'

'The other ten?'

'We avoided all improper haste. I asked for a gesture of our
utter intolerance of such a crime, but some of the council
believed that an example of compassion offered from a position
of genuine strength could be valuable, and his majesty was
convinced. As a younger man I might have held out for a higher
proportion of sufferers . . . '

'Five and five?'

Sidmouth couldn't smile at Hobhouse's accuracy. It hadn't
been the first defeat in his life, but it came like a symptom of his
vanishing faculties: 'The death sentence on the prisoners
Harrison, Cooper, Bradburn, Wilson and Strange is commuted
to transportation for life. A very mild alternative in my opinion
– no more than emigration to a warmer climate. There is no
substitute for death. They will be sent forthwith to Portsmouth
under escort for the next ship to Australia.' He paused again,
perhaps for a short prayer, then continued: 'For the remaining
five – that's Thistlewood, Tidd, Ings, Brunt and Davidson – the
sentence stands.'

Hobhouse said nothing. He made no notes, but he had long
ago shown that without them orders far more complicated than
the disposal of eleven criminals would be precisely followed. He
didn't ask for details, he only waited for them to come.

'To make the example more imposing the privy council
accepted my advice to order the execution for Monday
morning.'

'They have – we have thirty-six hours.'

'We can't complain.' Sidmouth spoke without conviction. 'I
did my best. I asked the council to let the sentence stand in full
severity. I'm not a man to interfere with a punishment that has
the sanction of many centuries. A traitor is drawn to his death
on a hurdle because he's unworthy to tread on the earth – the
earth he came from and will go back to. Ignominy is not
unsuitable for such a criminal. When I was young he would be
cut from the gallows while still alive and his entrails taken out

and burnt before his eyes. It shows how far we've come. There's a dangerous liberalism in the air. I don't like liberalism, it can be very damaging. Nine times out of ten it's cowardice and the tenth it's lack of principle. But Hobhouse, there are times when one stands alone . . . ' He must get the rest out quickly, to cut short the pain. 'Because of the inconvenience to traffic if they were drawn through the streets . . . '

'That part of the sentence,' Hobhouse said, 'will be dispensed with.'

'Dispensed with . . . ' For a moment Sidmouth was a defeated man, but recovered: 'We can expect a big crowd, I think. That is healthy. The sight of an execution has a beneficial effect. The most callous member of the public can't help remembering it. Nobody likes to be hanged like a dog, but when it has to be done it should be seen to be done. These liberals would be satisfied to have it done in private, but it wouldn't do for most people – for the working class or for many of the middle class. They would suspect some trickery behind the prison walls and might believe that the criminal had escaped. Besides, all of us who are in daily contact with the professional criminal can safely say that the dread of the public gallows is a strong deterrent. I would go further – it's a wholesome punishment. To abolish it would mean our recognition of the terrorist, and the law-abiding citizen would see that neither his property nor his life were safe. I needn't tell you, Hobhouse, on Monday morning . . . '

'There'll be the usual safeguards against disorder.'

'The usual safeguards – but Thistlewood isn't the usual victim. I'm not impressed by rumours of an attempt at rescue, but I notice a spirit of defiance which might increase between now and Monday.'

'There'll be placards ready, announcing that the Riot Act has been read and the people are to disperse.'

'More than that, Hobhouse – barriers must be put across the streets to stop the people at the back pushing forward too eagerly. Also a double barrier at a distance from the scaffold with only officers allowed inside. The fire brigade must stand by, and extra police sent to Newgate tonight so that preparations aren't hindered.'

'The army?'

'I dislike expediency. An infantry platoon in each street

leading to the scaffold will be enough. But not too close, in case of confusion. Provocation must be avoided, compatible with authority, and we must prevent any injury this time.'

'Artillery?'

'A field battery – out of sight, perhaps behind St Paul's.'

'The press?'

'It must be properly reported – but with tact, Hobhouse. One man only to be allowed inside the front barrier.'

'May I suggest a *Times* man? They've served us well.'

'I will speak to the editor.'

'And . . .'

'There will be no speeches from the scaffold.'

'Afterwards . . .' Hobhouse knew that one more decision of the privy council was being held back.

Sidmouth ignored him: 'You will be there?'

'It has been the tradition – someone from the ministry . . .'

'Thank you, it will be a comfort. I shall think of you at the time.' Sidmouth waited a moment. He was a master of delay and could still postpone the last revelation. 'I've always believed that no man is fit to be a public figure who cares a farthing whether he dies in his bed or on the scaffold.' His voice rose higher and thinner till there was a risk of it being lost unless he retrieved it soon. 'They're getting what they deserve. What is punishment but the emphatic denunciation of a crime? In these modern times it's a humane method. Quick and simple and certain. Quite painless to. If it's done smoothly, hanging doesn't really hurt.'

'Afterwards . . .'

'Afterwards?' Sidmouth tried to look perplexed, then with the suspicion of a sigh dropped his voice to an unusual depth, the tone he kept for profound regret: 'Ah yes, I see, the quartering of their bodies – that too will be omitted.'

*

The last two days of April, moist and bright, glimmered in the streets, over the roofs, in and out of the warm showers – in and out of the last two nights. A Saturday and Sunday of idle delight and gaiety, of opening expectation: two days of a London spring.

In Newgate the eleven men, wrists and ankles chained, spent Saturday in a state of numbed awareness, almost relief. The hard benches, small windows, jingling keys, boiled potatoes were the same as on any day of the past two months. The monotony and repetition were still there, hanging from the stone walls, haunting the passages, trailing into the yards, but no longer touched the condemned men. Suspense was broken, certainty had won. Each movement was checked by the rattle of an iron link, the twinge of bruised and bleeding skin, the throb in a swollen joint. The end of endlessness was marked by the knowing look in another prisoner's eye or the vibration in a guard's voice. A distance had grown between the eleven men and all others – a widening no man's moat across which they could never return. Familiarity was false, the old was new, even friendship among themselves was poisoned by the certainty of each man's isolation. Everything was the same yet fatally transformed.

On Saturday after supper the governor, with his chaplain and two sheriffs, visited the cells. The men were let out for him to read from a paper in his hand: one man to be detained during the king's pleasure, five to be transported for life, five to be hanged. The six to live were dismissed, the five to die remained. Thistlewood had drunk claret with this governor last week; Tidd's blush had become permanent; Ings had shrunk even smaller but kept his smile; Davidson held his Bible in his shackled hands; Brunt's ferocity was touched with a strange enlightenment, a hint of revelation. They stood, each between two guards in front of the officers, a dead silence over them. Not a flicker of agitation as the governor addressed them: it was his painful duty to tell them that he held a warrant for their execution on Monday morning.

A slight hiss escaped from the teeth of one of the guards, as if punctured by the shock, but the five prisoners never moved. They might be already dead. The governor hoped, trusted, that they would use the few hours left to them in this world in preparing for the next.

'The sooner we go, sir, the better,' Thistlewood said quietly. It sounded like a journey – they must settle up and pack their bags – and the others agreed: their wish was to die without delay.

The governor wasn't used to such impatience and warned them against frivolity. Their remaining life was short, and if they devoted it to repentance and prayer they could be sure that

117

God wouldn't desert them at the moment of fatal separation. But they didn't speak or make a sign. The governor said that the chaplain would help them prepare for the terrible change they were to undergo, or if they wanted a priest of any other acceptable religion it would be allowed. Not a word was uttered. Only Davidson opened his big mouth, but shut it quickly. The governor looked at each in turn, the sheriffs looked at their own feet, the chaplain looked at a silver cross on a ribbon round his neck.

Then Ings spoke: 'I want to ask, sir – may we be allowed to spend the rest of our time together?'

The governor regretted that it wasn't in his power. He could sympathise with their hope to cheer each other as only friends in this melancholy situation could do, but he had orders that they were to be kept apart. All he could grant was a last visit by their families on Sunday, and with his officers he marched away.

The men were locked in their cells, each with two guards. During the evening the chaplain returned to urge on them the prayers so humanely recommended first by the judge, then by the governor; to call them to contrition and humility before they could ask for mercy from the only source that might still supply it; to offer his own appeal to heaven for a revelation which could never come from the cold and cheerless speculations of infidelity; to warn them of the folly of rejecting Christian truth.

To four of them he was a tiresome little runt of a parson with a silly voice and a hopeless mission, but in the fifth his entreaties reached the withered nerves of an old belief. Late on Saturday night the chaplain told Thistlewood that the rays of wisdom had burst into the gloom of Davidson's cell, and in penitence he was seeking the pardon of his offended Maker and the safety of redemption. Thistlewood wasn't impressed and politely said so. He had long ago made up his mind about religion: the Cross had been supplanted by the Tree of Liberty. All he needed between now and Monday morning was a supply of snuff.

On Sunday the chaplain came again and tried every device of eloquence to persuade Thistlewood to follow Davidson and repent. With the black man's example how could a white man's heart not soften? Couldn't he be aroused to the perils of this dreadful threshold? Would he end the brief remnant of his days boasting of his impenetrability to Christian hope? Was he so infatuated with disbelief that eternity held no terrors? Did he believe he could rely on false heroism to support him on the scaffold and beyond? If Thistlewood would apply himself to the one faith from which true courage might be derived, instead of threatening to keep up this pretence even on Monday morning, it was certain that Tidd and Ings and Brunt would be converted too.

The chaplain failed. His custom was to preach in the prison chapel for the comfort of repentant criminals on the eve of expiating their crimes with their blood, but to the sorrow of his conscience, and of Davidson's soul, the others showed such disregard for the divine rights of Christianity that he feared some act of blasphemy during the service and cancelled it. He would rather not expose his holy religion to insults from such stubborn infidels. Thistlewood was quite agreeable.

*

. . . I see Monday morning though it's still Sunday evening.

Tomorrow is perpetually before my eyes whether they're closed or open. And in my ears, an incessant voice. It's everywhere – on the damp stone walls, in the stinking piss pot, in the sudden opening of my door, in the shock of a break in routine, in the dim nightlight that has been brought into my cell and will burn till tomorrow morning. *My* execution, the guards call it – my big moment. This evening it's the most important event of their lives too, occupying their thoughts as much as mine . . . I see it in their faces and the look they give each other. Knowing what it means for them as well as for me. A conspiracy of knowledge against me.

I rehearse it continually. Each time a clock strikes or a dog barks or a door slams I'm carried to tomorrow morning . . . I see myself walking to the scaffold, I can feel what it will be like. The sight of the gallows gives me a dumb electric shock. I have never seen one before, I don't know how it works. I'm gasping for breath, limp like an animal when I meant to be resolute – I am so ashamed. The guards support me, carrying me between them. Their rough hands under my arms, my legs dragging, my bowels opening. But in my disgrace I'm still conscious, I can examine the gallows with curiosity. A very English thing, not like a guillotine or a cross . . . I see the crowd shouting, 'There he is, that's him!' when I appear on the scaffold.

. . . I see the daylight surrendering to this dim lamp, the Sunday evening drawing in. The last of April. Thoughts come piling into my little stone box till there's no room for me. The last of life. To hang us is infinitely more terrible than anything we planned. Worse than any murder. A man with a pistol pointed at him, or in agony from poison or having his head battered in, can hope to the very end that he will survive. Hope makes death easier. But the certainty of not escaping is our final torture. I can't endure the last humiliation without going mad.

I wonder what the other four are doing . . . I see them through the walls, thinking the same as me. But this is the right way to finish up. All wearing prison clothes, crawling into identical boxes, watching each other suspiciously, knowing that we feel the same. It has been the pattern of life all through, it's the true end – every man inside his little cube, pretending to be different from the next. Even the king's palace is a prison with guards round him and the same fawning and hypocrisy.

. . . I see the insult intended in these chains and the swollen painful flesh. But it's the man who offers the insult who is degraded. An iron fetter worn in a just cause is more honourable than Lord Sidmouth's gold watch chain. I feel no guilt, I shall die in peace. A crippled conscience would be as incurable as a lost life. There may be things I regret – moments of thoughtlessness, secrets buried in me as in any man – but the thing I'm to be killed for, the ideas and passions which rule me, don't need excusing. They purify me and will support me in this last fulfilment. They are the spirit of my life, to accompany it to the end. It was a celebration, not a crime, to obey that spirit. It would have been dishonest to do otherwise. If I refuse to repent, it isn't through pride or self-love or any evil in me. I have never been a bad man. I only feel castrated, deprived of manhood, of responsibility. I'm no longer master of my destiny, but its victim.

. . . I see, through the walls, the peewits on the winter fields in Lincolnshire when I was a boy.

. . . I see the barrier of pity and embarrassment that divides me from the world. I stand outside it now. When men look at me they see a purple face and a broken neck. But my overwhelming, growing need of survival defies them. It shrieks

at me from all sides. Before Friday afternoon I didn't care what
happened. I was still the man I had always been, with a mind
full of fancies which I tasted and developed or discarded. Each
new hour, each new minute had its own ideas. My imagination
kept its youth, it revelled in the variety of choice. I was free to
think what I liked, indifferent to the verdict and the sentence –
they were irrelevant while I was a living man. But since I was
told I am to die I have had only one thought, one hideous
unconquerable idea. I'm alone with it, flattened by its weight,
frozen by its permanence. It's always here like a ghost beside
me, solitary and jealous. It's everywhere, on the walls, in the
patch of sky through the window, in the eyes of the guards who
sit with me. It gnaws at my solar plexus, banishes all rivals,
hovers over me, shakes me with icy hands if I turn away or shut
my eyes. It flies in pursuit when I drive my mind to escape. It
spies on me all day and lies in bed with me at night and steals
into my dreams. When I wake it waits a few delicious trembling
seconds for me to believe that it was a nightmare before
crashing back into my cell, into my head, the prison of my skull.
It sounds in the voice of anyone who speaks to me and mixes
like a chant with my own words, whatever I'm saying. At that
moment on Friday afternoon a revolution happened. Nothing
was the same as it had been the moment before.

Since then I have been a dead man. As if I didn't know, one of
the guards told me so this morning. He wants to put a bet on a
horse on Tuesday, the day after my execution, and believes that
from another world a hanged man can watch a race before it
happens. I can appear to him before the start and tell him
which horse will win. It'll be no bother for me, he said, and I
might like an excuse to return so soon. Monday evening would
be the best time. He isn't afraid of ghosts, he'll be expecting me.

I hate these distractions – a visit from the governor or the
chaplain, or a change of guards. They talk to me, they won't
leave me alone. They believe that because I'm to die by a law of
man's, not of God's, my death is unlike anyone else's, unlike
their own. All men, all their lives, are condemned to death but
have indefinite remissions of their sentence. I'm no different
from them, or from what I was before Friday. I happen to know
the limit of my life, so am saved from ignorance. They should
envy me, and stop talking to me. To be cheerful they start a
conversation about sport or politics or women, or suggest a

game of dominoes. The fatuous, belittling dominoes we play! I only want to think. I never look across my cell without meeting a guard's eyes.

But I love these men who sit with me. I seize on their friendship, fasten on their little jokes, cling to their condescension. Last night I woke in a fright of being left to face this thing alone, and looked to make sure they were still here – my last friends, faithful to the end. They won't abandon me. They're concerned for me, not just from duty, and I should be grateful. I love the governor too – his good manners and soft words and flattering eye. Like a good hotelkeeper he asks if I have all I need, and hopes there's nothing to complain of. I'm to be brought whatever food or drink I like, and books and paper. I should be honoured by the kindness I'm shown, the civilities I was never paid before, if they didn't underline the purpose. A condemned man is a prince. They will give me everything on a velvet cushion, except the rope. I must be fed and kept alive for my death tomorrow morning.

. . . I see the ridiculous chaplain coming every few hours with another automatic speech. He has done it for so many of us before, and there will be many after me. I'm the same as the last or the next – a candidate for the scaffold, a number in his total. He says nothing I can feel, nothing to touch me with tears or happiness, nothing from his heart that can enter mine. Only vague recitals to suit all condemned men in general. Not a look in his eye or a note in his voice to show that he wants to understand.

. . . I see Susan and Julian when they were brought this afternoon. It didn't last long, I was glad when it was over. I should have preferred not to see them at all. The embarrassment, the wondering, the weeping. They were stripped to their underclothes and searched before being allowed in. They too are to be punished. A widow and an orphan by act of law – for doing what? For being mine. I am an enemy of society, but to my wife and son I'm what I always was. Yet transformed, as a sheep is transformed into mutton.

I told Susan that I didn't want to die but I would rather be hanged twenty times than be Edwards or Adams and live, that I have no fear of the moment of death, I only fear the fear which will come before. I said that one doesn't suffer, it's nothing, an easy way, one is stopped in the middle of a thought, one falls with an unfinished idea, squeezed out by the rope, strangled before completion. It was inadequate, not what I meant to say, but how was I to behave? I looked to the guards for help, but they shuffled and looked away. I told Julian that they were going to kill his father for the good of the country. He flung himself at me and had to be pulled off. Crying, shouting, tearing at the guards' clothes. Take him away, for God's sake! It's the sight of my son that unmans me. Poor boy, I wish he hadn't come. The look on his child's face as they dragged him out, of horror and love and an emptiness more miserable than any pain – I shall remember it all my life. *All my life*, all sixteen hours of it.

Susan too, at the end, lost her reason. Her gold hair took fire, she shouted of murder and justice and vengeance. Vengeance! Suddenly I resented her and was impatient for her to leave. She could tell me nothing I wanted to know, give me no help, only shout or whine or choke. She was no longer Susan but a symbol, an actress playing a part. It's the same with me and the rest of us – the governor, chaplain, hangman, even Lord Sidmouth. We are puppets dangling at the whim of some nameless horror, propelled by an unimaginable machine. Nobody can control it. We have no choice between good or evil, truth or falsity, so it's useless to think of taking action. There's no signpost to anywhere, nowhere to go, nothing to fight. Susan stood there and tortured herself with the shame of her weakness. I could hear the unspoken words that filled her head. I didn't love or hate her, merely wondered how I had admired her so much. I saw then that I had never liked women, and Susan had lost the identity that kept her from the rest. Only men count now, and perhaps they always did. I have never been in love, I never had time. It's for aristocrats and poets. For me, women have no importance. I have taken them to bed, except Clothilde. I have married two of them and said I loved them, but it wasn't true. Now lust has died in my body before the rest. I must squirt the vitality that remains into the shrivelled, shrunken corpse of my life.

. . . I see pretty factory girls in the north of England. Necklaces, ear-rings, bright clothes. Singing and giggling at their work. A jutting hip, a straining bodice, a lovely smell of treachery. What tricks could those lips and fingers play?

After Susan and Julian had been taken away I felt like a dog that creeps off to die by itself. Now every quarter of an hour makes me a year older. I am only forty-nine but catching up quickly. In a few hours I shall be an old man . . . I see the old man I would have been if I didn't have to die tomorrow. The one I was always to become. As a boy I had a vision of myself with a bent cracked body and white hair. Old Arthur Thistlewood, the man they hanged one Monday morning, the first of May.

. . . I see somewhere an English road I walked along, between the rich fields. There was a cottage through the hedge with roses and honeysuckle and a garden beside it where a man was digging. He stopped to look up and wave as I walked past.

. . . I see my cock as I use it – not many more times – for the foul piss pot in the corner. Never for a woman again. But it hasn't done me badly. Better than I deserve, perhaps. It had ambitions of its own which I didn't keep. And it will stand up once more, I have always heard, when I'm twisting in the pit. One last erection, a spurt of fertility in death's eye. But it won't be mine . . . I see the event clearly. The crowd and governor and hangman and chaplain. I even see the death of the four men beside me, but I can't see my own. Up to the last moment of life, but not beyond. My death grows closer, it approaches and vanishes on the instant of its arrival. Courage can deal with imprisonment or torture, but is unnecessary for death. Death is too elusive to be faced. If I try to look further, if I watch my body on the rope being cut down, it isn't mine but another man's. There's nothing of me to focus on, or focus with, once my feelings have stopped.

*

A sound of carpentry came through the barred windows, hammering and sawing all through Sunday night. By torch-light London prepared for the last drama of English justice tomorrow morning, the first of May. A stage was being put up for a special performance and given full publicity. Stands were erected behind the barriers, but by midnight the ten-shilling seats were sold out. Touts traded on the rarity of a five-man execution. Places in windows were snapped up at two pounds or more, depending on the view. Pubs stayed open all night for the show – the festivity, with its urgency and horror. Workmen whistled, drunks shouted, loud hammer strokes reached the prisoners inside Newgate, beating out the seconds, minutes, hours. Curses and complaints came from men with years to live – with a life before them – and the hum of a crowd collecting, the excitement flooding with the dawn, the cry of a man selling hot sausages. There was a prison governor for stage manager, snatching tots of brandy and bouts of sleep between visits to the work. And for impresario, a dry old man in bed in Richmond.

The five men to die also slept soundly, it was said. The guards said it to each other and counted the hours till dawn, the clocks striking the numbers the men would never hear again. Three gone for ever, four gone for ever. A cock crowed too soon and the daylight came in. The two guards in Thistlewood's cell listened to him grinding his teeth in his sleep. They said it was time for a cup of tea, in a whisper so as not to wake him, but he turned over and said he'd like one too. They were putting a kettle on, he was just in time. Time was the thing. Time, time – a lifetime ahead. He asked if it was nearly time, and they said there was no need to get up yet, there was plenty of time. They offered him snuff, but his head was lined with it, he had too much, he would leave some for them in the cell. They suggested a game of dominoes, or paper to write a letter – there was still time. They were only trying to be cheerful. He got up and lay down, and got up and walked four steps back and forth, and watched the guards watching him. They never took their eyes off him. He lay down again and listened for the clocks. Five gone for ever. He fell asleep for a few minutes and jumped up, lost, not knowing where he was. He must have been dreaming, he looked so happy for a moment. They told him to get dressed, then shook his hand: they were going off watch and wouldn't see him again. The last two came in to take over, and also shook his hand.

At six o'clock the chaplain visited the prisoners for one more effort on behalf of his Redeemer – their Redeemer too, if they would believe him. Only Davidson believed. The black man took the sacraments and joined the chaplain in prayers for mercy. The other four refused politely. Then on an impulse Brunt took a glass of holy wine and drank the king's health. Davidson added the royal family to his prayers.

Little Ings said to the chaplain, 'You can send my body to the king for turtle soup.' To his guards he said, 'May Day – there'll be plenty of people out this morning. Been up all night to get good places. The fuckers, they've got no guts.' On the first of May last year he had brought his family to London.

They were given their own clothes instead of prison uniform. Davidson was content to be separated from the infidels, he didn't want their company on his lone path to eternity. Brunt asked if they could have breakfast together and word was sent to the governor, but he couldn't allow it: probably they wanted to encourage each other and settle what to say on the scaffold. Better to keep them apart as long as possible.

'Just as I always thought,' Brunt said, warmed by his glass of wine. 'The happiest morning of my life.'

They ate breakfast alone in their cells with the guards watching. Their appetites were good, it was said. Porridge, bacon, fried bread, mugs of sweet tea and an orange each – a gift from the old man who had been in court. He came to the prison gate but wouldn't leave his name.

*

. . . I see a pub where I once stopped for the night, and the supper of pork and potatoes that was brought to me in the bar.

. . . I see myself as a child. But I am still that child, a laughing healthy boy again, with my life in front. I have never grown up. My life is crammed into these last hours. My whole existence lies in the diminishing time, growing smaller till it disappears. All the variety, contradictions, muddle of thought and fact are being compressed. But now I'm indifferent to my life, I don't care what happens to it, I'm not sorry to die. I have wasted too much time in idleness, delusions, ignorance. Too often I didn't know how to value life while it went on. I cheated my own heart. My life is a hopelessly insignificant one, with no moral in the way it ends. Somehow I must justify it in these remaining hours, and find a purpose for it. But I'm exhausted. Scorched and withered by the intensity of these days. I have no emotions left. I'm impatient with fatigue.

I want to tackle this idea. This thing. Touch it, handle it. I want to face it boldly but I don't know what it is. I look beyond the scaffold into the future – *into this morning* – and speculate till my mind aches with uncertainty and aversion. All I can see is that it has no comfort or meaning. It's an infinity of nothing, non-life for ever, and so doesn't exist. But I can't accept that. I strain to discover a secret, and when I don't find it I invent my own fantasy to put into the vacuum. I believe I am going somewhere, I neither believe in my annihilation nor in somewhere new. This afternoon I shall still be in the familiar world – in Lincolnshire or Paris, on the platform at a London demonstration, even in this prison cell. I shall not desert the old places.

*

Suddenly the tramp of boots on stone. Louder and louder, marching down the passage, coming this way. The governor with his two sheriffs, a squad of guards and the hangman – a grey little man with wide shoulders, long arms, an air of reassurance and trust. His assistant was the same but younger – his son. Also in the party was a young man in a smart London suit, perhaps a civil servant from the ministry or just a young man with influence who had asked for the privilege of attending. Lastly the chaplain, softly mouthing the ritual for the dead.

'*I am the resurrection and the life, saith the Lord.*'

The marching stopped outside the five cells, the doors were wrung open, the men stood up. Rising to be killed, sinking inside. Then the swift and brutal pinioning, the trapping of a man's arms, the snatching of his last free movement. The two hangmen dodged behind him, grabbed his elbows, pulled them backwards, tying them in agony with a strap.

'*The Lord gave and the Lord hath taken away.*'

In the next rough moment the man was spun round, pushed back on the bench for his chains to be knocked off. A quick hammer at the rivets, a ringing of iron, and the links fell from wrists and ankles to the stone floor, chiming like bells. Hoisted to his feet, reeling and sick, his stomach dropping out. Frog-marched out into the passage.

The five men stood outside their cells, arms hitched behind them, shoulders hunched to the point of deformity. Each with an orange in his hand, one with a silver snuff-box. The governor's party faced them. Thistlewood's lean face was rigid, paler than ever. He didn't smile but bowed slightly: 'I am ready, sir.' No more claret together for them. Then he turned the bow into a contortion for his nose to reach the hand that held his snuff, like a bird scratching a broken wing. He would be composed, master of himself.

Tidd, next to him, also bowed, his blush still growing. Ings ignored the governor's party; stood stiffly in his butcher's clothes with an old nightcap on, trying not to look so small, and gave a nervous laugh. Davidson, struck by a great emotion at the sight of the others, struggled to fix his dark eyes on the chaplain's lips.

'*Lord, let me know mine end and the number of my days.*'

At the end of the line Brunt nodded to his friends and before anyone could stop him dived forward to shake their hands heartily in turn. An awkward, twisted grabbing of hands. It was too much for the smart young man who swayed on his feet, reached to steady himself against the wall, then decided he had made a mistake and walked quickly back the way he had come. The warm morning, the close stale air in this prison passage, would make anyone faint.

'Well, Mr Thistlewood,' Brunt said, 'how d'you feel?' To the limit of his pinion he performed the bizarre flourish with which he had once waved Thistlewood to a chair.

Without smiling Thistlewood said, 'Never better,' and took more snuff.

Brunt said again, 'It's the happiest morning of my life,' with his back to the officers standing in embarrassment. To Tidd, convulsed with a fit of choking, he said, 'Keep your spirits up! All will soon be well.' Tidd bit a hole through the peel of his orange.

Then an odd thing began. A murmuring in the air, a whisper growing in the ears of the governor and his party and the five prisoners. An unearthly growl from inside the old stonework of Newgate. The foundations were groaning under the weight, or the prisoners of past centuries – ghosts with their ageless death rattles – were returning to protest against this early morning outrage. This early morning of spring, the first of May. The noise grew quickly, rolling and swelling through the building, deafening and unstoppable. A chorus of a thousand men – thieves, debtors, bigamists, embezzlers, rapists, swindlers, murderers, scapegoats, radicals – were offering a lament for the last short walk of five friends, an angry requiem on this day of wrath and pity. Locked in their cells they stamped on the floors, drummed the doors and window bars, banged their mugs and piss pots, roared, cheered, wept. The prison was full of an invincible disgust, a clangorous flood of shouts and tears and love.

One of the sheriffs said sharply, 'Come on there.'

Brunt shouted, 'God bless you all!' But for a moment the fury of the prison population stunned his cheerfulness, and he fell sullen and morose.

The governor jerked them into action. The procession, led by the sheriffs, started through dark passages filled with a great din from the cells. The guards struck the doors with truncheons as they passed, and shouted, 'Stop it!' which added to the noise. Ings' nightcap fell off, the hangman's son picked it up and pushed it into the young butcher's hand. The governor coughed and blew his nose, pretending he couldn't hear or see. Through it all, like a thin tune blown on a reed, came the chaplain's voice chanting from his book.

'*For man walketh in a vain shadow.*'

Thistlewood followed the chaplain, deaf to the prayers and the noise, his eyes fixed emptily ahead, seeming abstracted and unaware. Tidd was also silent, but stumbling and more affected, showing less manlinesss than he would have liked. He had rehearsed this a hundred times in the last three days, but it wasn't what he had expected. Ings cheered Tidd on with laughter, swinging the nightcap in his hand in a fit of bravery or a delirium of fear. Davidson, his eyes lifted and hands clasped in front as far as the pinion allowed, tried to catch the chaplain's words.

'*And now, Lord, what is my hope?*'

Brunt, recovering from the other prisoners' outcry, joined in the racket to show that he hadn't, as he felt, left his guts behind in his cell.

The journey wasn't long enough. They would have walked all day through the gloomy prison, they would have walked round London to stretch the distance. And nothing escaped them. Each sight or sound was tasted, cherished, adored and clung to. The sheriffs led slowly, but too fast. Round corners, down flights of steps. A sickening descent, a reeling in the eyes, the bursting noise in the ears. Through the last doorway and out into the sunny prison yard, across worn flagstones to the gatehouse. The blinding daylight after the dark inside. The noise from the cells followed the procession, streaming down the walls from the pattern of little windows. Behind each was a man beating out his anger. One of them, with a voice like a trumpet in his stone sound-box, sang, '*O give me death or liberty!*'

Ings forced a burst of laughter, then switched it into a piercing echo: '*O give me death or liberty!*' He repeated it again and again, madly: '*Death or liberty!*'

Walking across the yard behind the chaplain Thistlewood looked up at the sky and said, 'What a beautiful morning.'

From the windows of the governor's house a lady with her friends and children watched the little band march into the gatehouse. The gates swung open for them to pass through into the street, and shut heavily behind. Five men who had once been locked in were now locked out. The fury of the other prisoners was trapped inside, muffled behind the walls. But outside the gatehouse where the procession halted a new noise met them – the noise of free people.

The crowd was the first thing. Five pairs of eyes and ears feverishly registered the last details of this world. All London was out there – a thousand people, ten thousand, with their holiday talk, their delight and dread. Half were women, many were children, a few were drunk. They stretched away down the streets and out of sight, this hopeful May Day morning; filled the windows and lined the balconies, perched on a fountain, clung to lamps and drainpipes, chattering and expectant. As Thistlewood observed, it was a lovely morning. Could London ever look brighter?

At news of the little band coming from the gatehouse a tidal wave rolled back across the crowd: 'Ah!' Faces turned, opera glasses were lifted, voices rose in a thrill of satisfaction, then dropped nearly to silence. Some people clapped for the five men lined up in the sunshine, their shoulders hunched by the pinions and each with an orange in his hand. Thistlewood in his blue coat with velvet collar, the others in working clothes – one more job of work to do. A woman shrieked and a man shouted, 'God forgive you, gentlemen!'

Infected with his new song, flicking his nightcap in time, Ings bellowed, '*O give me death or liberty!*'

Thistlewood's jaw twitched, his mouth stayed shut. He hated this pause and the sun was in his eyes. When the chaplain asked once more if he would accept the rewards of repentance he shook his head impatiently: 'But remember my behaviour. I'm perfectly happy, I shall die at peace.' With difficulty he took more snuff and tried to suck his orange; then clamped his lips tight again, frowning at the sight in front.

The second thing, after the crowd, was the scaffold. Across ten yards of cobbles – a high platform with a ladder. A black curtain nailed round it, to hide the works. A strong beam over the platform, between two posts. Everything was new. The hangman stood on a chair to tie the last of five ropes to the beam, while his son spread sawdust over the boards. In a corner lay five coffins, the lids propped beside them. They looked too small. More buckets of sawdust were passed up and emptied into the coffins.

The chaplain continued to entreat the prisoners. Soon, too soon, they would be ushered from that scaffold into the presence of their God.

Brunt said, 'If there is a God I hope he'll show more mercy than you buggers did.' The chaplain tried to show him pity, without concealing his contempt.

Ings laughed: 'Well done, Brunt!' and screamed his song: '*O give me death or liberty!*' Someone in the crowd took it up.

Brunt shouted, 'That's right! – better to die free than live like slaves, the way you lot will.'

Tidd said nothing, but quivered through his body. He had seen that scaffold as a boy. Davidson leaned back against the gatehouse wall, his lips calling for the intervention of his Redeemer. '*Deliver me from all mine offences.*' The chaplain stood close to him.

One of the sheriffs went forward to lift a corner of the black curtain and speak to someone behind it. The hangman chalked five crosses on the platform under the ropes. The sheriff signalled to the governor. A bell rang somewhere. They were ready for the first man.

'*Hear my prayer, O Lord!*'

Thistlewood was ready too. For an instant a look of unequalled misery entered his face, bottomless and so incomprehensible that it seemed to astonish even him. In surprise and panic his eyes flew everywhere, swivelling in their sockets like pebbles rattled in a box. He turned and gave a wild imploring glance, as if expecting to see death behind him. Then his eyes stopped, caught by some inner power, and lodged rigidly ahead. His face was calm again, his body stiff. Treading the straightest path he could, but unbalanced by his pinioned arms, he walked over the cobbles to the ladder. Two guards helped him up. On one of the steps he faltered and took it again. The last climb of a man, shortly to drop the same distance. At the top he crossed the sawdust to the edge; bowed to the crowd and surveyed the sight; blinked and peered, hoping to see someone he knew. It was like this on Spa Fields, standing on a wagon with the people thick under the trees. Here they were kept beyond the barrier, too far away to hear a speech or for a rescue if he had ever believed in one. A murmur reached the scaffold like the sea washing over a rock and broke into a small cheer, then fell back with a gasp, leaving a single catcall.

Without a word, at a command from nobody, the men in the crowd took off their hats. A church clock struck a quarter to eight. Thistlewood might hear it chime the hour.

*

. . . I see the crowd down there. Women and children, and the men's bare heads. A boy crying to be taken home. Brought to watch five men falling off a stage. He thought it would be Punch and Judy, but the puppets are real today. Ten thousand faces, twenty thousand eyes have come to see us drop. The same people who came to hear me in Spa Fields. Some of them I know. I called them my friends but now I'm not sure. I hate them. Or I love them. Once they loved me, and they can't hate me now. They could save me but they don't. They'll stand there in their shame and talk about me this afternoon. They won't say they knew me, only that they came to see me die.

Whispering, waiting. Not one of them will die today. Nor need I. I'm not ill, there's nothing wrong with me, I could go on for forty years. Healthy and strong. Just dying from a fatal illness given me by my friends. Painless but incurable. How many other men will die today, who thought they would be here tomorrow? A few in beds somewhere. Not enough of them, for me. I wish the entire crowd down there could die, and millions more. Knowing that the world will be destroyed today and those people will be dead would make me happy. I shall get there first and wait for them. Today, not later. In Fox Court one night someone said that the people had been dead for years. But they will live for years. Those men and women and children will be alive tomorrow, just like today. There are men down there who have made engagements for next week and will keep them. I could have made engagements too.

They watch me looking at the sky, they tell themselves that I'm kissing it goodbye or praying. The sky up there, going on for ever. Lucky, lovely sky. No cloud, no wind, no bird in it. If I could fly . . . I see beyond the crowd, beyond the streets and houses to bright green trees, spring fields, earth, flowers, roads, ditches. They will never be mine again. The simplicity of this. And the impossibility. It won't happen. But it will. And yet it can't.

I'm trying to be cool. It's the hardest thing I have ever done. Not every man could be so cool. I have little feeling – am I a man at all? Soon I won't be. The minutes creep. It was twenty-five, then twenty, fifteen. I don't know how many more. Will nobody stop them? Have I no friends? Am I despised? Rejected? I had two friends, a beetle and a tree. The beetle shared my cell these last few days. No man would do that. And a piece of tree showed through the window. A beetle and a tree were my only friends.

. . . I see myself. Half of me is observing the other half, the brave watching the coward. There are two of me, myself and I. And I love myself. To love anyone I must love myself. It isn't self-pity, though God knows there's cause for pity now. But I can look at myself as another person, my lifetime partner, the person I shall never leave. I shall stay with him to the end.

. . . I see myself at the foot of the ladder. I began to cry. I couldn't stop it. I am a strong man and I sobbed. The blood drained out of me, my legs collapsed, something choked in my throat, I was already being strangled. But it was fear, not the rope yet. My reason left me. I wanted to sit down and shut my eyes and wait. Be sick or disappear. My life fell round me like a house. I would lie down and drown in tears. A great longing for solitude flooded me. To die is a private thing and I would do it alone. *My* death, to be done my own way. A man's most intimate act, turned into a public show. Somehow I got up the ladder. My dread was to faint at the top, but thank God I didn't. More likely to have a brainstorm. The machine was running out of control. Sparks, overheating, a continuous scream. My head rattled with the ideas, visions, sounds that filled it. They chased each other at speed, assaulted the one consistent pivot that transfixed my life, but couldn't obliterate it. It was impossible to faint, I was sustained by that pivot. It would last to the end, under a barrage of unfinished thoughts.

. . . I see the hangman coming forward, greeting me on his scaffold. This is his territory. A host with a friendly welcome for the first guest . . . I see the policeman in the loft at Cato Street, coming at me with a rope. The man I killed.

*

The grey little hangman and his son worked expertly, wasting no time; led Thistlewood under the beam to the furthest rope, positioned his feet on the white chalk cross, slipped the halter over his head. His face was flushed and anxious without a trace of fear, while they tightened the knot under his left ear; then a tall canvas hood – he asked them not to draw it down over his eyes yet, he would watch the world to the end. A murmur of interest passed through the crowd. From the top of a house someone shouted, 'God Almighty bless you!' and Thistlewood gently nodded, held up his pinioned hands, one with an orange, the other with his silver snuff-box, and clasped them together. Once he had been free to tie his shoelaces, comb his hair, wipe his nose. Now his mouth was contracted in a sort of smile.

A reporter from *The Times* stood among the officers below the scaffold, scribbling in a notebook. Thistlewood spoke to him: 'I hope you'll believe that I've been sincere in everything I did. You can put that in your paper.' The man's pencil worked fast. 'Tell the world that I died a friend of liberty.'

The hangman signalled to the governor with his sheriffs by the gatehouse. It was Tidd's turn. Desperately he turned to Ings. In a wild sing-song Ings cried, 'Give us your hand. *O give us death or liberty!* Goodbye, old friend.'

Tears burst from Tidd's eyes, his chin dropped, his mouth opened to wail like a child: 'My wife and daughter . . . '

Ings pumped his hand: 'Don't droop, old cock, it'll soon be over. Revenge is all it is – what's wrong with revenge?'

Tidd tried to smile, choked on his tears, wrenched his hand from Ings and scuttled to the ladder. His foot caught in it, his legs failed, he fell on the ground. The guards held him under the arms, supporting him to the top. He ran to the mark on the platform next to Thistlewood and stamped his feet in agitation. The crowd cheered his eagerness for the rope. He bowed, his tears drying in the morning sun, and waved to a woman shouting from a window. He knew her, he would show he was at ease. He wanted the knot slid forward under his jaw, for a quick clean job, and wriggled to get comfortable. Like Thistlewood he wouldn't have the hood pulled down till the last moment, and stood sucking his orange with a look of calm and contempt. Tidd would never speak again.

Little Ings next. He ignored Davidson, praying with the chaplain, but shook Brunt's hand: 'At last we'll find out this great secret,' and laughed. 'Remember me to the king, God bless him!' he cried to the governor. A guard told him to get going and the butcher marched briskly to the ladder; bounded up it and began kicking and jumping in a frantic dance, skipping over to the coffins: 'That's mine in the middle – the smallest,' and spat into it; then turned to the crowd, raised his pinioned arms and gave three savage cheers for liberty. Half mocking, the crowd roared with him. As the hangman led him to his place Ings shouted, 'Goodbye Smithfield!' and kicked a foot towards the meat market. He wanted extra rope for a longer fall, being the lightest, and asked for his nightcap under the hood. 'Listen to this and put it down,' he shouted to the *Times* reporter. 'I die an enemy of all tyrants and spies. This is what's left of James Ings. You see the last of an unfortunate man. Put that down!' He looked up at the rope, laughed with derision and began again: '*O give me death or liberty!*'

Thistlewood, beyond the silent Tidd, said, 'Shut up, Ings. Can't we die without this noise?'

Ings only laughed.

A woman shouted, 'Be firm!'

Ings shouted back, 'Firm! – but we have children, madam.' And sang again, more quietly.

Davidson was different. With the chaplain beside him muttering holy syllables he trod the cobbles to the ladder, showing nothing but humility. '*O spare me a little, that I may recover my strength before I go hence and be no more seen.*' At the top, without glancing at the five coffins or the three men tied to the beam or the two empty ropes or the crowd, and without ceasing to pray, he bowed to the hangman and his son and let them do their work: it was almost a joy to submit. They pulled the hood over his eyes and down to his nose, his purple lips moving with the chaplain's: '*Lord, thou hast been our refuge from one generation to another.*' The chaplain was content: one out of five had bid adieu to a world he inhabited no more, and was preparing for the unknown country he was about to enter.

Alone by the gatehouse Brunt began to rage: 'What's this? Why am I left to the last? They can only hang me once – are they afraid I'll make a speech?' To the others on the scaffold he shouted, 'What's it like up there? How's the view? Don't go without me – I'm coming!'

One of the guards tried to control him: 'Why not do the same as the black man? – ask God's pardon.'

'Why the fucking hell? I've done nothing. What do I want pardon for?'

'That's what you say. But any harm you've ever done to someone, or anything on your conscience – you ought to ask God . . .'

'I haven't got a conscience, I never hurt anyone.'

'But you've got a wife and daughter. God will forgive you . . .'

'My mind's made up, I've made my peace.'

'If you believe . . .'

Brunt couldn't stand it: 'Wait for me – I'm coming!' With a lunge he rushed to the ladder and flung himself up on the platform like a trooper storming the enemy. It startled the hangman but roused a cheer from the crowd. Brunt saw a man down there he knew: 'Good morning, old friend! – I hope you enjoy your breakfast,' and fiercely jerked his head towards the coffins.

Little Ings, in the middle of the five, stopped singing: 'All my friends have come. On the roofs – look.'

Someone shouted, 'See you in the White Hart tonight!'

'A game of cribbage!' Ings shouted back. 'We'll play for drinks.'

'In that window there,' Brunt said, 'you see the lord mayor of London.' Then a flash of metal beyond the crowd caught his eye, a glint of a bayonet in the sun. 'What? – soldiers!' he shouted. 'Why all the soldiers? I see, I see – a military government's the only thing for England. It needs more men like us . . .'

'It won't be lost – what we've started,' Ings said softly, and began to hum, '*O give me death or liberty!*'

Brunt shouted to the crowd, 'Don't you wish you were coming with us? It's a privilege – there's nothing to look forward to if you're left behind. Come and join the party, it'll be fun.' But his levity was collapsing, the old scowl slipped across his face with the halter: death had him by the throat. Though not as tall as Thistlewood at the other end of the line, Brunt was the bulkiest of the five and began to diminish quickly. He didn't weep or tremble, but grew smaller, paler, more absent. The flesh shrank from the bones of his face to leave a skull with staring eyes, a mask locked in a livid grin.

Five men standing on a platform in a row and sucking oranges, each tied by the neck with a rope to the beam above: the last cord joining them to life, as the umbilicus had been the first.

*

. . . I see a small brown stain on the hangman's shirt – a clean shirt today but the stain couldn't be washed out. I love this man who hammered off my chains and attends me now. He knows what to do, he has done it often. I need him, I am a beginner and he can show me how. I never learnt a skill like his. I love his warm fingers on my neck as he adjusts the rope – the contact of another man, the last to touch me. I don't remember the first. He's deft and gentle, not from friendliness or irony but from experience. It's the way to do it – nasty work and he wants me to co-operate. He'll be pleased when it's over. So will everyone – then they can go to breakfast. Just now I asked him the time and he told me, but I've forgotten what he said. Perhaps I never asked. I can feel his breath behind my ear. At home he has a wife, and keeps pigeons or a dog or goldfish. And he has a son! Not much older than my Julian. Helping his father to kill men. Death is his living. He lives by it. *Lives*.

To live! To live as a convict like the other five, transported to Australia where they can sleep and wake and breathe. To be imprisoned for *life*. To be condemned to live – in a dungeon, a cage, a barrel, on a rock in the ocean with no space to sit or lie down, surrounded by darkness and solitude. To live standing on this white chalk cross with a rope round my neck for a thousand years, for eternity. To live, no matter how!

. . . I see the point of life with extraordinary distinctness. It is to be a man. Each minute is an age of happiness. It isn't too late, there is an infinity ahead. The others must be tied up first. My life is before me – five minutes of it, or four. I don't know when it will happen or what it will be, but there's still so much to do. Four minutes are a wealth of time, a life to enjoy. Time to look and think. I have such clarity and wisdom now, I know all the things I should have said and done. I don't do them, I'm wasting my life, I always did.

I love the people down there, though I despise them. They want to watch this terrible transition into darkness, to learn from it and be ready when it comes. Are they laughing and yelling or are they silent? There's a great noise in my ears, but a noise of nothing . . . I see a girl at the front of the crowd. She makes me so tired. Once I would have smiled with a small warm hope. Her bright eyes, teeth, neck. My body is betraying me. But I live in it, it's all I have.

There can be only a minute and I haven't begun to do the things I meant. I have forgotten what they were, I only remember myself. I never knew how much I loved myself. And my son. I was going to organise my life, arrange it better. Give me those three minutes back! Give me life again! I would use every moment, waste nothing, make an eternity of it. If they bring a reprieve, if this is a joke or a dream . . . I see sweat trickling on my nose and feel it in my eyes – the sting of death. I'm sweating for the love of life. Sweating with anger, I've never been so angry. They should do it now, not keep me waiting. I long for it, this instant.

The hangman's shoes squeak. It will be the last thing in my ears. I have to count them as they pass – the last time I put my clothes on, the last crap, the last breath. A horse has emptied its bowels, dropped a heap of dung close to me on the scaffold. I heard it and now I smell it. Or perhaps it's Tidd. At the back of my skull I feel an itching, freezing, sucking emptiness that grows colder and greedier from second to second. I like it, it is my death – my very own. Through it I feel the heart-throb in my neck against the prickle of the hemp. And I smell soap as well as shit. They rub soap on the rope to make it slip, they think of everything.

. . . I see the sun on a window across the street, flashing a message in the glass. There's a message for me, a future in that light. It will absorb me, I shall rise into it and disappear.

The impossible, unbelievable awfulness of this thing . . . I see Tidd's death beside me, but mine is hidden round one last corner, under one more skin . . . I see something hanging in the pit down there, below the chalk cross I'm standing on, but it's a dummy. What will I become? I am a man and I shall be someone else. Who? And where? And when? How long have I got to find out?

. . . I see a froth of spit on the platform. One of the others shot it there. But none of us has fainted. We are being honourable, I think. We haven't renounced any convictions or repented for any crimes. We stand together, each alone and wrapped in the same terror. If I could reach I would put out my hand to touch Tidd. My neck is paralysed, I can't turn to see him, but I feel him there. I love Tidd. I have more pity for Tidd than for myself. I'd like to show him, but my arms are strapped. I can hardly get the orange to my mouth or the snuff to my nose. The pinion is for when I'm hanging, to stop me grabbing at the rope . . . I see myself pinioned by Lord Sidmouth's men when I was thrown out of parliament . . . I see another froth of spit beside the first. But I have none in my mouth, my swollen tongue rasps on my throat. I can taste the bacon grease from breakfast, but it doesn't soothe the dryness . . . I see the plate of food they brought this morning. The first mouthful fell from my lips but I must have finished it, I saw the empty plate. The last meal. Now I've sucked everything from my orange, there's only an empty skin. I've lasted longer than the orange. Robespierre's orange. But my coat is darker blue than his. My God, will nobody put a sponge of vinegar to my lips?

The sun on the window is brighter. Brighter than the eyes of the girl in front . . . I see the head of the beautiful lady-in-waiting carried on a pike, and her body being dragged behind.

. . . I see Lord Sidmouth's face down there, I would know him anywhere. He's writing in a notebook, reporting for *The Times*.

*

The reporter filled page after page. The hangman and his son made last adjustments. The chaplain, thorough in his way, couldn't leave the men alone. A hitch would be a disaster and one day he too would get the final summons. To each he promised that even now he could guide them on the long journey, and begged them in their remaining seconds to seek deliverance from eternal death.

Thistlewood said, 'No, no – I don't need your help.'

Tidd shook his head without speaking, resenting in his eyes this intrusion on a man's last moments.

'You'll give me a good character, won't you?' Ings cried, and tossed his half-sucked orange at the chaplain.

Grimly through his teeth Brunt said, 'I've done all I need for where I'm going.'

Only Davidson prayed, joyful to be on his way to that great Being who at a word could hide a man's iniquities for ever. '*A thousand years in thy sight are but as yesterday, seeing that is past as a watch in the night.*' The chaplain took the black man's hand in his own for a moment, then let go: they might drop together into the pit. Perhaps it wasn't a long journey at all.

The hangman pulled down the hoods. As he did so, as if his fingers called it up, a dead silence landed on the crowd.

Thistlewood had to stoop.

'Now, old gentleman,' Ings said, 'finish me off tidily.'

The reporter strained to catch the words.

'*We bring our years to an end, as it were a tale that is told.*'

The ropes were checked again, to make sure they were free and wouldn't catch.

Someone in the silent crowd called, 'God bless you, Mr Thistlewood.'

Thistlewood's hood slightly inclined.

Someone in a window said, 'Keep straight, Arthur.'

'That's it, Celia – keep straight,' Ings said, but his voice wobbled at the end. A year ago today he brought his wife and children to London.

A woman at the front toppled over on the cobbles in a faint. The sun was getting warm.

Below his hood Tidd's lips moved, but no sound came out. He had seen it all before, when he was a boy. The orange fell from his hand and rolled off the platform.

Brunt kicked off his shoes: 'I shan't want you buggers any more.'

The reporter wrote it down.

Davidson chanted: '*Thou knowest, Lord, the secrets of our hearts.*'

Ings said, 'Now we'll know what makes the stars shine,' and began his song, '*O give me death . . .* ' but couldn't go on. He remembered the five who were on their way to Australia. Now he knew why the convicts he used to see in Portsmouth harbour, being taken out to the hulks, went so cheerfully.

'*I heard a voice from heaven . . .* '

Eight o'clock chimed.

The hangman and his son shook the pinioned hand of each man, and saluted the governor and sheriffs; then ran down the ladder and dodged behind the black curtain underneath.

'*Blessed are the dead which die in the Lord.*'

*

. . . I see the crowd out there, though my eyes are covered. Hats off for the people, but a hood for me . . . I see Robespierre's face the moment before the end . . . I see my own face reflected inside the canvas. But I had blindfolded myself, I don't need it over my eyes. I don't look into the darkness any more, there's nothing to see. The others are dead already, I am the only one alive. The only man in the world, alone. How can I believe in my death? I hear somebody breathing. Is it myself? I'm asleep and this is a dream. They're waiting for me to wake up, they've put the kettle on. Once I dreamed I was being hanged. It wasn't like this. I hear a kiss. A soft kiss quite close . . . I see Davidson's fat lips on the chaplain's silver cross . . . I see the cross I'm standing on, but nothing beyond. A kiss in the Hôtel de Moscovie one night. There will be one more kiss. Something has got under my skin, crept through me and grabbed my stomach. My stomach has turned over and fallen out. Dropped into my trousers. Blue trousers. Wet and filth. What are they waiting for? My God, my God, a reprieve . . . I see a small boy in Lincolnshire, climbing a tree and stealing apples.

*

A loud sob spoilt the bright morning.

The *Times* reporter stopped writing and looked up.

Another woman fainted, but the girl at the front with bright eyes never took them off the five blindfolded figures.

Thistlewood stooped again for a pinch of snuff.

A scream split the hushed crowd: 'For God's sake don't leave them there – turn them off!'

Other people took it up, shouting, 'Turn them off . . . !'

Davidson reached out blindly for the chaplain's hand, but couldn't find it.

Under their hoods five men's living minds were assailed with thoughts known only to themselves, though anyone could guess.

Quietly Thistlewood said, 'I see . . . '

The chaplain stepped back.

*

Thistlewood jerked several times, each fainter than the last. After a minute he hung straight, twisting slightly. Tidd hardly moved after the drop, his death was the swiftest. Little Ings struggled a lot despite the extra rope he had asked for: the hangman and his son had to swing on his ankles with all their weight. Davidson, after three or four spasms, was motionless. Brunt suffered worse – two guards were called to help pull. But in five minutes all was still: not a twitch in any of the ropes.

Alone on the platform the chaplain read the closing words: *'We give thee hearty thanks, for that it hath pleased thee to deliver these our brothers out of the miseries of this sinful world.'* He came down the ladder to join the governor and sheriffs. The gates opened, the party disappeared into Newgate, the gates closed. The reporter from *The Times* looked at his watch: time to go for a coffee, but perhaps he should stay. Better not risk missing something. The crowd waited. There would be an epilogue.

Half an hour after the drop the hangman and his son went back up the ladder with two guards. One after another they lifted the legs, swung the bodies out of the pit, sat them on the edge while the ropes were cut from the beam, then dragged them across the platform to the coffins.

The reporter watched the next part carefully. Decollation was the word, and it was rare these days. People were becoming sensitive: the judicial maiming of the dead was considered medieval. Soon it might be obsolete, like hurdling and quartering. Already it was hard to get a man to do it. But the ministry had found one. He came from the gatehouse with one of the sheriffs, quickly up the ladder: quite young, with long hair over his collar, though he hid his face under a mask tied with a scarf and kept his hat pulled down. He wore the loose white coat and trousers of a hospital orderly. One hand rose compulsively to tug at the scarf across his chin.

A block of wood was passed up and put at the end of the coffin. The first body was laid on its back in the coffin, shoulders lifted to the edge, head over the end, neck on the block. The rope was untied, the hood removed, the shirt turned down. Strangulation had brought a violent purple to the face, shocking to anyone who hadn't seen it before, but there was

142

little distortion of the features.

At the sight of the masked man putting a surgeon's knife to the bare throat the crowd gave a shout of horror. For a moment he was put off and looked up, but the sheriff waved him to continue and in a minute the head was severed: an anatomist couldn't have done it better. The hangman took it by the hair to the corner of the platform and held it up for public execration: 'This is the head of Arthur Thistlewood, a traitor!' It was greeted with hissing, hooting, noises of disgust, but not for the treason. With less confidence the hangman did the same at each corner, then put the head into the coffin with its body.

The reporter wrote it down. The edge of the knife had been turned by a bone but the masked man had a spare one. When he put it to the next throat the crowd howled again. Someone yelled, 'Shoot that murderer!' but he pulled his hat down and tightened the scarf. Tidd's head was bald, with no hair to grip: the hangman held it by the ears. The masked man worked with speed as the crowd grew angrier: curses and jeers and groans. Ings bled heavily, Davidson gaped on an unfinished prayer. Each time the hangman was treated with more loathing; he gave the last – Brunt's great scowling head, the most altered of all – to his son who dropped it. The crowd saw it roll into the sawdust: 'Butter fingers!' The masked man slipped away, in a hurry to get out of sight. Justice was over.

The reporter watched the coffins being carried back to Newgate and looked at his watch again: almost nine o'clock – an hour and a quarter since Thistlewood went up the ladder. The authorities should be praised for sparing the culprits and the public a prolonged ordeal. On his way to the *Times* office he began composing his story for tomorrow's paper: '*The history of one of the most horrid conspiracies to disgrace the annals of our country was terminated by the removal of its ringleaders. The perverseness of their minds, blinded by envy and revenge, deluded them with the idea that if their work of murder was completed a career of power lay before them. The whole nation had been horror-struck by their plot, but their true character was only manifest on the scaffold, where they were seen for our edification rather glorifying in what they had attempted than repenting of their crime. It showed to what extremities Englishmen, when excited by political passions, are capable of being led. May the example of this morning's ceremony teach us those lessons of prudence, good faith and obedience to the laws of God and man as might conduce to our individual happiness, the*

143

stability of the throne and universal safety of mankind.'

The crowd scattered, the stands were taken down. The scaffold was to be left all day under guard as witness to the event, and dismantled at sunset. Children were allowed to cut shreds off the black curtain for souvenirs, or finish sucking the oranges. It was May Day, a public holiday.

In her drawing-room not far away the Russian ambassador's wife, Princess Lieven, wrote to her lover, Prince Metternich, in Vienna: 'The conspirators, Thistlewood and Co., were hanged an hour ago, and at the moment the streets are full of music, of drums and of people in masks. It is the festival of the chimneysweeps, and they are dancing at every corner. It makes me sad. Do not imagine that I regret the fate of Thistlewood; I feel pity for these poor human beings, for these aberrations of mind and imagination. Why did Brunt die crying, "Long live liberty!"? Why did that emotion dominate him at the moment of saying goodbye? Even in him the emotion is not criminal. I do not believe in the existence of a human being evil at heart; that would be to doubt the Creator. A false exaltation – such is the motive of crime.'

*

Monday morning was saturated with its usual replenishment. The clocks were wound up for seven more days, the prayers and hymns of yesterday's evensong filled the minister's head. There was no fire in the grate today, it wouldn't be laid till autumn. Sunlight slanted over the floor, shadows of young leaves played on the furniture, even the Whitehall traffic rolled more lightly for the first of May. It had never looked so pretty out there. Lord Sidmouth lingered at the window, enjoying the bright English spring that fell through the glass and warmed his trousers.

One of the evening hymns, evocative of the approaching dark yet bearing a promise of future blessings, had rung with him this morning all the way from Richmond Park to the office: '*I hear a voice you cannot hear, which bids me not to stay. I see a hand you cannot see, which beckons me away.*' Through the carriage window he caught a woman's eye, that told him she had heard him singing. As the words came round for the hundredth time he was struck by a sudden unsummoned whim, rare and free and perfect like the morning, which he hadn't had for years. In the past he had stifled it before it could touch his conscience. Now he felt a shiver of guilt, or delight.

He stood at the window for ten minutes, which he had never done; then for half an hour – unthinkable before today. The Doric clock over the empty fireplace struck eleven. Usually he was at work by half past nine, but today's duties had been dispatched much earlier. He deserved a day off, he would devote it to literature. There were passages of the journal to be polished and new ones to be rehearsed. One of them was urgent.

At last he went to the desk and took the proper stance: '*He hoped he had been of some use to England. He believed he had.*' The words came fluently, he knew them by heart. '*So far, at sixty-two, neither the faculties of the mind nor the functions of the body had warned him of declining vigour, but by listening to that faithful inner monitor he perceived the wisdom of retiring before the eye was dim, the hand weak, the spirit broken. While his energies retained full power he could divert them from the trivial concerns of this life to the momentous interests of the next.*'

This would be a good moment to be interrupted. He should have thought of it before he began. He went on: '*When his official bed was strewn with thorns he could never have deserted it, but now that it had become comparatively a bed of roses . . .*' Comparatively – but there would always be work: letters to the papers, privy council meetings, audiences with the king, interviews with journalists and young politicians. '*With the success of his arrangements for the country's security he might be justified in asking the king's permission to surrender the seals of office into those hands which had bestowed them so trustingly, and be released to enjoy tranquillity.*'

He came to the point. Some things were hard to put into writing: with others he needn't try. Though his children had done their best to comfort his widowhood, they were a disappointment. Perhaps it was this that revived the desolate, lonely feelings he had suffered after his wife's death. '*While still in office he had no time to consider it . . .*' If he hadn't declined an earldom he would have a better chance, and better choice, for a second marriage. '*On retirement he might seek again the sympathy of mind, communion of thought and feeling which he had found nowhere else but in marriage, and which for the last nine years had been so cruelly lost.*' The promise of spring roused a twitch of life, almost a twinge, in Sidmouth's flesh and drew his lips into the slenderest smile as he copied the paragraph into his journal, then rang the silver bell.

'Well, Hobhouse.' The syllables banished the smile, and with it the brief vision of a second Lady Sidmouth.

Hobhouse brought two papers. One was a letter to the king, forwarded from the palace by special messenger.

'It seems to be addressed from a public house.' Sidmouth took it delicately as if to avoid fingerprints or contamination. 'The signature is Susan . . . ' He cut short and looked up. 'It's none of our concern but she might take advice as to changing her name.' He read the letter: 'She most earnestly entreats his majesty to grant one consolation, by restoring to her the mutilated remains of her late unfortunate husband so that she, his majesty's loyal petitioner, may shed a silent tear over him before he is consigned to the tomb.'

Hobhouse kept the second paper, knowing better than to interrupt.

'We have no cause to aggravate the condition of this lady.' Sidmouth felt touched with charity today. 'It's enough to reply that compliance would be contrary to established usage.' He tried to remember a proverb, or invent one, but failed: 'I've never understood what the doctrine means, Hobhouse, that human life is sacred or how it can be proved.'

Twisting his legs slowly round the chair Hobhouse waited for any further utterance, then passed the other paper over the desk: 'From the governor of Newgate.'

Sidmouth read it out: 'The coffins of the five traitors executed this morning were filled with quicklime and the lids screwed strongly down. A trench was dug alongside the underground passage leading to the cells and the coffins placed in it, in line. They were immediately covered with earth and finally with stones. We may be satisfied that no trace remains for any future public observations.' Another smile, more wry than the earlier one, crept into his face. 'In our reply to the widow we may add that compliance would be attended with great inconvenience.'

Hobhouse saw that the matter was closed, to be committed one day to the journal which he would read for himself, though he could anticipate it accurately. He prepared to leave the room, but was stopped at the door.

'And Hobhouse,' Sidmouth said, 'ask my coachman to be ready, will you?'

Alone in his office this fine spring day Sidmouth was

146

suddenly overwhelmed by a desire to get out, away from these sombre walls and the pervasive, tortuous spectre of the secretary. It was an attack he hadn't had for years and only rarely in his youth: an instinct that an old ambition was to be fulfilled, an assignation kept. He had trained himself to be suspicious of impetuosity, to resist a sudden fancy, but for some reason which he didn't care to define this was exceptional. The day ahead was free.

Five minutes later he walked out into Whitehall and got into his carriage. To Parliament Square, then to Westminster Bridge – he opened the window and told the coachman to drive along the river. A midday brilliance, to confound the smell of sewage, shone among the boats plying between the bridges. It was a comfort to be in the heart of the empire, at the source of so much that was beneficial and profitable to man. Lulled by the springing and upholstery Sidmouth crossed his legs and allowed his contentment to be stirred by a vague excitement.

Past Charing Cross, Adelphi, the Temple, Blackfriars – but he couldn't sit back for long. Driving through London he felt a need to make some personal devotion, a thanksgiving at a private altar. Or why not a public one? – the sunlit dome of St Paul's swelled brightly above the roofs. Sidmouth told the coachman to drop him at the steps and wait.

Inside he was at first blinded by the dark. Moving over the chequered floor he began to see familiar shapes, pale arches, the glint of distant brass, the shimmer of a window; slowly up the nave, penetrating the cathedral till he arrived under the dome, and stopped. The choir was empty but the organ played, throbbing in the pillars, casting music to the furthest corners, rolling over him like the breath of God. He sensed the fitness of the place and of the spot he occupied, exactly under the enormous crown, and stood there alone for several minutes, reaching in his mind to touch the walls, roof, crypt, the whole shell of God's majestic house. He was at home, belonging as surely as the Englishmen who inhabited tombs and chapels, or lay in bronze on catafalques or sat enthroned in stone, in robes and togas and laurel leaves. At their feet knelt common soldiers, sailors, children, heathens; above them hung flags stitched with battle names; on their plinths were written the facts of power and glory. It was proper that Sidmouth should stand among such men.

147

A lesser Englishman distracted him: he wasn't alone with God and the organ music. Among the people – a pair of vergers, a choirboy tidying the books, a few worshippers left over from the morning service and tourists piously murmuring in wonder – was a young man who caught Sidmouth's eye by the peculiar nervousness of his movements; who dropped to one knee for a quick prayer, crossed himself, sidled through the cathedral, a dim figure in a brown coat with hair to his shoulders and a pale beard which he kept tugging, drawing attention by trying not to be seen.

Sidmouth wouldn't have noticed anyone so ordinary, but a youthful insolence attracted him and drew from his memory, where it had been lost for nearly thirty years, the shadow of another young man of the same age and class: an intruder in parliament when he was speaker, who let out a squirt of abuse and blasphemy from the public gallery and was quickly stifled. There was nothing to connect that one long ago, who would now be middle-aged, with this one in St Paul's, but Sidmouth believed in some rule of Providence by which every trivial happening had a purpose in the bigger scheme.

Though usually he ignored strangers he was compelled to watch. The young man bowed towards the high altar, looked over his shoulder, turned into one transept, checked himself and turned into the other. He stopped at the gate of a small chapel as if for another prayer, but changed his mind again and walked quickly, keeping near the wall, to the side door of the cathedral.

Then Sidmouth saw the woman. A pretty woman probably, though her face was hidden by gold hair under a shawl, with a strong air of purposefulness. She stayed in the side aisle and was followed through the shadows by a boy; slipped behind one pillar, was joined by the boy, and passed to the next; looking out into the nave, searching for somebody in the cathedral, she didn't know where.

Sidmouth stood rooted in the middle. He knew at once that the young man and the woman were linked. It wasn't his business, he had come to worship privately and give thanks, he didn't care about these people's affairs but couldn't disregard them; could only submit to a plan drawn by a higher authority. He must watch, and was glad to be alone.

The young man had vanished. The woman was still there,

with the boy behind her, moving quietly behind the pillars. Then they too passed out of sight. A momentary shaft of sunlight: Sidmouth saw the side door open and close behind them.

He had never been so fascinated, almost petrified. What they were doing was dimly perceptible in his mind – the horror and sacrilege and animal brutality of a human deed. He felt ashamed and honoured to be a witness. He stood there, his feet nailed to the marble floor, his body chilled to stone. Minutes went by, an infinity of time in which no thud or cry or gasp reached him – or did they? His transfixion was ended by some other power, not his own. When he could move, he turned and walked slowly over the cathedral floor. His track was laid out. Between the pillars to the side door.

The instant he was out of the door he saw it. The sunlight blinded him as the darkness had, but he knew where to look: he might have put it there. In the shade in the corner of the porch. Brown coat, long hair over the collar. The young man lay face down where she had stabbed him. A small dark pool of blood on the flagstones caught the sun. Sidmouth thought of a clock that had run down because nobody had wound it up. It had stopped on Monday.

He had no idea how far the woman and boy could have got. Stepping with care he turned out of the porch, down the street to where his carriage was waiting. He wouldn't have lunch today, but drive home to Richmond and send the coachman back to Whitehall to say he would be at work tomorrow. This afternoon he might lay spring flowers on Lady Sidmouth's grave.